# SILENT
# ENCHANTMENT

## Lacey Dancer

A KISMET™ Romance

 **METEOR PUBLISHING CORPORATION**

Bensalem, Pennsylvania

For Kate Duffy and her staff

Thank you for caring as much about the author as the work.

## LACEY DANCER

Lacey Dancer is a woman of many interests. Her husband and writing are numbers one and two; but that doesn't stop her from collecting antique salt cellars, an assortment of farm animals and learning organic gardening. Roses and peonies are her favorite flowers and weaving words into dreams of love the best way to earn a living.

# _____ PROLOGUE _____

"Well, how is it this time?" Alexander Kane demanded as he pulled on his shirt. These yearly physicals were a pain, but necessary. His father had died at fifty from a heart attack. Alex knew what stress and pressure could do, especially in his business, so he suffered through having his schedule messed up once a year while Brian poked and prodded, X-rayed and examined every part of his anatomy after taking half his blood for a bunch of tests no one but a doctor could understand.

Brian Matthews, his friend and doctor, replaced the blood-pressure device and turned to him. "No better than it was last year. In fact the diastolic is up five points," he said bluntly. "And it won't get any better if you don't quit burning your candle at both ends. When I told you to start taking periodic

breaks from your hectic life-style and to reevaluate
your priorities I meant just that. Instead, what do
you do? You go hellbent for leather at the vacation
spots with a sexy woman who expects to be enter-
tained on one arm and a briefcase full of work
tucked under the other. That is not what I meant
when I said 'vacation.' What is it with you? Do
you have a death wish or something? Or are you
just incapable of relaxing for more than a second?''

Alex scowled. Few people but Brian would
have had the nerve to confront him this way.
''You know what the computer business is like. I
either keep ahead of the pack or kiss my company
and my professional life good-bye. I didn't work
my tail off for that.''

Brian's eyes narrowed at the sarcastic tone.
''You aren't the only one who worked to get on
top and busted his buns to stay there. No one gave
me the reputation I have in this city. But *I* have
sense enough to know that a well-tuned body like
a well-tuned car runs a lot longer and a lot better
than a neglected machine. And you, my friend, in
spite of a few days on the ski slopes of Aspen and
maybe even a week on the beaches in the Bahamas
qualify as a clunker. Your blood pressure is hover-
ing just under the hundred mark. Your ten pounds
overweight—not that it shows yet. Your choles-
terol and triglycerides are up and I wouldn't give
you a nickel for your chances of lasting the year
without an ulcer or something worse to your
credit.''

Alex stared at Brian, reading the disgust and the truth in his eyes. His temper died as the words sank in. "That bad?"

Brian sighed deeply and nodded. "That bad."

Alex frowned, his mind hunting with computer-like logic for an answer to the problem. "I really thought I had a handle on what you told me. I took time off I really didn't have at regular intervals. I cut down on the hours at work and I stopped going to the office both days on the weekends." He finished buttoning his shirt and slid off the examining table to tuck the tails into his slacks.

In his stocking feet he stood two inches above Brian's six feet. Auburn hair was made even darker in contrast to his fading tan. Brandy-colored eyes showed an unusual hint of bewilderment. "I don't know what else I can do."

Brian leaned against the wall and folded his arms over his chest. "Why not try a solitary change of pace? Forget taking one of your ladies with you and go off by yourself. I have a place in the country where I go just to lie around, fish, and do nothing. The peace and quiet refreshes my mind and gives me a chance to unwind."

"You? You're a city dweller like me. I can't imagine you in a country setting."

Brian chuckled, his green eyes alight with amusement at Alex's surprise. He dug in his pocket to pull out his keys. Selecting one from the small ring, he detached it and handed it to Alex. "Why don't you try it? You might like it.

There are no phones, no one to bother you, no traffic, and no smog. Take a few days and relax. Really relax. Get nine hours of sleep. Eat regular meals, minus the salt, and following the diet I'll give you. And don't take any work with you. In fact, if you can, take a week. Maybe at the end of that time you'll have your priorities straight and you'll know how to reduce the stress in your life.''

Alex took the key, wondering why he was bothering. There had to be another way. Rural pastimes were not his domain. He didn't even own a pet and never had. "I don't know, Brian."

Brian pushed away from the wall, his expression turning serious. "I had hoped a suggestion from one friend to another would work, but I guess it won't. I'm telling you as your doctor, use the key!"

"But I have this deal . . ." Alex started to argue.

"I didn't expect you to be able to go today, but soon, very soon."

Alex left Brian's office, unable to forget the gravity in his friend's eyes at the results of his physical. He had been so sure he had gotten on top of the stress problem. It wasn't often that he failed at anything he set out to do and to know that he had done so with an issue as important as his health left him feeling off balance, angry and privately humiliated. He left the medical-complex building so deep in thought that he didn't notice that the skies had opened up to deluge Atlanta with rain. The first inkling he had was the feel of cold water drenching his head and shoulders.

He swore, glaring up at the sky and getting a face full of water in the process. He ducked his head, yanking his suit jacket up to afford a little protection as he dodged across the street to the open-air parking lot where he had left his car. By the time he was inside he was wet through to his skin. Swearing again, he started the car and turned on the heater, getting cold air to add to his discomfort. His stomach tightened with each oath. The reaction to tension and problems was so common that he barely registered the acid ache. Easing into the late-afternoon rush-hour traffic, his curses increased in frequency and vehemence. First it was the driving rain that was making visibility almost impossible. Then it was the man weaving in and out of traffic that had almost seared off the fender of his brand-new Porsche, and the final straw was the tractor-trailer rig that was sprawled across all five lanes of traffic on his side of the median. The accident took two hours to clear. Neither his temper nor his stress level improved through the process.

By the time he reached the entrance to his underground parking building, Alex was hungry, his stomach sore, and his head felt as if it were in a vise. He was in no mood to discover that somehow between his home, his office, and Brian's he had lost the security card to raise the gate barring his entrance. It took twenty minutes and three trips around the block to find a parking place on the street in front of his apartment building. Soaking wet, he rushed passed the security guard sitting at the front desk and headed for the elevators. They, at least, were empty and ready to take him to the top floor. Not bothering to get a raincoat, Alex grabbed his spare card and left.

"With my luck one of them damn car-parts thieves has probably stripped my Porsche by now," he muttered to himself as he stalked across the lobby, almost slipping on the marble floor. "Damn rain," he added as he stepped out into the downpour. His car was intact even if his temper wasn't.

"I need a hot shower," he mumbled, beginning to shiver when he finally reentered his apartment. "And a large brandy."

He got neither. The brandy decanter was empty. The shower was cold, icy cold. He shot out of the stall, too furious to even think of new swear words. It was then he saw the note his housekeeping service had left on his nightstand.

"Hot water heater seems to be acting up. Suggest you have plumber check it out." Alex shrugged into his heaviest bathrobe as he read the note aloud. Stopping only long enough to sneeze, he grabbed the phone and dialed the first plumber listed in the phone book.

"I don't care how much it costs," he raged a moment later as the indifferent voice on the other end explained the emergency rate for a house call. "Just get a hot-water heater over here."

He listened for a minute, his expression darkened to an alarming degree. If the plumber had been there he would have thought twice about arguing. "What do you mean you can't?" His fingers clenched around the receiver. "How can you run a business without stocking parts that break down?"

Another excuse. "I don't care how much space one hot-water heater takes. I don't even care if half the damn city is without hot water. I do care that I am getting pneumonia standing here freezing my butt off talking to you." He inhaled deeply, his breathing in short-tempered gasps, feeling his head pounding, a sure sign his blood pressure was taking dead aim at the moon. The acid built in his stomach causing real pain to add to his headache. Suddenly, he had enough. Anything, anywhere was better than this.

"Never mind. I'll try someone else," he decided through clenched teeth. He hung up and then dialed the building manager, explaining the problem and apprising him of the fact that he would be out of town for a week. The idea of escaping the city and all its aggravations sounded like heaven. Next he called his secretary to cancel his appointments.

"Tell Lark, Inc. I had a personal emergency and that I'll be available for a meet mid next week. If they want that new design for their software, they'll wait. Otherwise we'll just find another buyer," he said, unable to stiffle a sneeze which his secretary heard and commented on. "Of course I'm all right, if you don't count maybe catching the flu. I'm just tired and I've decided to take a few days off. I'll call you when I get back."

Alex hung up the phone and tossed some clothes into his suitcase. Brian's house had to be better than a hot waterless apartment. The simple country life sounded almost perfect. Or it would have been if he had not gotten royally lost in the backwoods of rural Georgia ninety minutes out of Atlanta. Alex stared at the tiny sign declaring that he had just entered Tyrell's city limits. He was supposed to be in Burkeville.

"City? What city? One lousy service station, a food mart that has seen better days, three churches, a combination police and fire department and a law office. Oh, whoopee, a stop light and a doctor's office, too." He stopped at the light. "This is not where I'm supposed to be. Not only am I in the wrong little farm burg, but I am taking up talking to myself on a regular basis. Brian, you don't know what you started with your little bombshell." His eyes narrowed as he eased down the street. His headlights caught the sign proclaiming a bed-and-breakfast house. His head still ached, although not as bad now. He was past hunger and well into starvation of the first order. And he was tired, too tired to continue or to care whether he ever found Brian's house. One one-horse town had to be as good as another for getting away from it all.

# ONE

Lorelei Starke stood at the open window of her room, staring at the swirling gray mist shrouding the land. The moisture-laden air clung to her skin, touching her gently, teasing her senses with promises of the day to come. By midday the sun would burn away the delicate clouds to reveal the lake, the trees that fringed it on one side, and the house that had been her home and refuge these past nine years. She inhaled deeply, savoring the subtle scents of the night flowers hidden by the mist. Mystic would be waiting. She had no time to linger if she wanted to ride in the fog. Limping slightly, she moved with a strange grace to the closet to pull on a pair of light-gray jeans and pale-lavender sweater. Her dark hair hung to below her waist, a silken fall without a hint of curl. With practiced ease, without the benefit of a mirror of which there was not one in her room, she braided her hair in one rope, tying the end with a narrow length of ribbon. Her boots were black, worn enough to be comfortable. Taking a banner of rainbow silk from the peg on the wall from which fluttered many such pieces, Lorelei swirled the scarf about her head and throat to ward off the slight chill she knew lay in wait for her beyond the warmth of the house. She crept downstairs, careful not to wake her aunt. She slipped outside via the back door. Sound and sights were muffled or hidden making finding a direction in the eerie stillness of the dawn difficult. Familiarity with the grounds guided Lorelei's footsteps safely to the stable where Mystic waited.

She greeted the Arab stallion with a touch. He returned the greeting with a soft nicker. The saddle and bridle slipped on easily, and in moments, Lorelei was astride the gray stud and easing out of the yard toward the path to the lake that both knew by heart. The mist accepted woman and horse, wrapping them in a protective cocoon. Lorelei rode silently, feeling the rhythm of Mystic's smooth gait sink into her being, demanding her concentration and her strength. On horseback, the limp that made her less than she once had been was forgotten. Her slender body was poised, truly a creation of beauty and power born to catch the eye and stir the senses. Once she had touched the hem of fame, stood before audiences, accepting their adulation as her due. But no more. The limbs that had been her joy to move, her delight to stretch to their limit, were damaged now beyond repair of human hands. Her life, that part of her existence, was gone just as the mist would be when the sun burned it from the embrace of the land. Now she lived in the shadows, for the sun had become her enemy. She shunned humankind, for they felt pity for her. Her mind and the wonders that it could perform had become her source of strength and power. No audiences shouted her name. Few but Pippa and Lorelei's family knew how she spent her time in the room tucked away under the spreading eaves of the house that had sheltered her from the curious when she had turned away from the only life she had known. Dreams for what would never be were tucked away now in the dark pages of her mind. The child who had lost everything in one tragic accident had become a woman who preferred shadow to light, silence to speech, and stillness to movement. What could have shattered some had simply tempered the steel that had been honed with the life she had lost.

Alex turned over in his bed, glared at the clock on the nightstand, and swore. Maybe his friends were right. Maybe moving to the country had been a little extreme. Even Brian had doubted his intention to make so drastic a change. Six months ago he had stumbled across the sleepy little town of Tyrell, cursing his luck, the impulse, and storm that had stranded him in the backwater. He could smile now, remembering the way he had discovered his hideaway. He had gotten lost again just trying to find his way back to the main road. He had turned down the only paved lane he had come to. Ultimately it had led to one of the worst drives it had ever been his misfortune to encounter. His Porsche had almost not recovered from the bumpy road with the clay mud that had resembled the Red Sea minus Moses. Mired up to his expensive hubcaps in blood-red goo, he had approached the house standing on the hill to use the phone not realizing the place was vacant.

By the time the real estate man had come by to plant the For Sale sign on the grounds, Alex had been more than glad to accept his offer of a lift back to town. His car had been towed out of the mud and to the only garage in town for repairs by the agent's farmer brother while Alex had waited at the agent's office. His stay had been lengthened to five days while the parts necessary to repair his Porsche had been ordered. In that time he had begun to see what Brian was talking about. Something about the sleepy burg had gotten to him. He could feel tension seeping out of his body. Determined to alter his life-style while he still had a life to alter, he had given into his first impulse ever and made an offer on the old house.

When the deal was closed he had been back and forth from Atlanta to Tyrell enough times to realize that the ride, now that he knew his way, would not be prohibitive to him residing in the country for a while, at least until he repaired the damage he had done to himself. After all, if a few days could bring a measure of relief, then a temporary permanence would be even better, he decided. So despite his friends', including Brian's, raised eyebrows and comments questioning his sanity, he had hired a team of local men to put the place in shape. He might have bought a hideaway in the country, but he had no intention of roughing it. The electricity and plumbing, plus an auxiliary hot water heater, had been renovated, the house and grounds repaired, cleaned, and painted, and in the last two weeks his computers installed and the new furniture delivered. This was his fourth night in the house, and so far he had yet to get one decent night's sleep. The place was too quiet. Even the bed-and-breakfast where he had been staying when in town had had a bit of noise from the other guests. It was so silent here he could almost hear the grass grow and he could definitely hear the snores of the dog he had impulsively picked up at the local pound.

The sound of a soft whine made him peer over the bed to the mutt lying on the floor. "I knew getting you wasn't a good idea. It's amazing what silence and sudden loneliness can do to a man." Already the damn animal had him trained for all the little tasks that went with having a pet. "Why can't you need to go out at a decent hour? It's barely light.'' He crawled out of bed and stumbled to the cahir where he had laid his pants.

Impulses. He had never given into them in any form and here he was falling victim to more quixotic decisions in the last six months than he had made in a lifetime. Brian had said a change of life-style was called for. Alex had more than followed his orders. The house was no mistake as it was within reasonable driving distance to the city, he assured himself. And he'd get used to the quiet and the dog. He glanced at the hopeful canine face tracing his every move and sighed deeply.

''I never knew I was a sucker until you came along.''

The dog jumped to his feet, his tail wagging, clearly undisturbed by the aspersions Alex was casting on his character.

''Come on, Dog,'' he mumbled, leading the way downstairs. ''You know I never intended for you to sleep in my room. And furthermore, you and I have to find you a name that you'll answer to. I can't keep calling you Dog even if you do wag your tail every time I say it.'' Alex opened the back door, glaring faintly at the fog that came swirling in. ''Don't get lost, you hairy thing,'' he called as the animal ran into the gray mist and disappeared. ''You'll probably end up in Michigan and I'll end up stepping into that lake trying to find you.'' He attempted to peer through the murk and then gave up with a shrug. Closing the door, he put on the coffeepot and then went back upstairs to finish dressing. Bare chests might be manly, but it was a damn sight too cold and, besides, there was no one to notice his new ten-pounds-lighter physique.

He returned to the kitchen a few moments later, expecting to find Dog scratching at the door to be let in for breakfast. "Blast you, mutt," he grumbled, seeing no four-foot creature with soulful eyes waiting for him. "I need my head examined." He stepped outside, feeling immediately disoriented as he called repeatedly for the animal without getting any response. He left the door open and went back inside to pour himself a cup of coffee. Still no dog. He walked back to the porch, calling again. By the time an hour passed with no sign of the mutt, Alex knew he would get no work done until he found him.

Shrugging into a light jacket, he muttered a few curses, most of them aimed at his own stupidity. "I'll probably get lost and that fool will be sitting on the porch when I finally find my way back," he predicted irritably as the fog swallowed him in its damp embrace. Keeping his eyes alternately trained on the well-trod path that began at his back door and the blank wall of gray in front of him, Alex made his way carefully in the direction of the lake. If he stayed on the path he should be all right. Every few feet he stopped and called.

Finally he reached the lake. The path continued toward the thicket. Deciding to risk going farther, he followed the trail. The fog was better when he entered the trees, becoming less dense and even patchy in some spots. The trail, however, started to dwindle to nothing but a trace of footsteps strewn with roots and rocks. Stumbling, muttering, Alex pushed on. He wasn't sure whether it was his own continue-until-you-succeed personality or the need to find the dog that drove him. All he knew was that he wasn't going home without Dog.

Lorelei entered the thicket, almost sorry to see the mist clearing a little. She liked the gentle stroke of the moisture on her skin and the silence. Suddenly Mystic jerked up his head, his ears pricking forward. Lorelei reined in, listening. Then it came. The sounds of another voice, a deep, ill-tempered rumble that rolled over the land like distant thunder. A frown chased across her brow. She glanced back the way she had come. She had no desire to meet anyone this early in the day. Suddenly there was a grunt of pain and a distinctly heard, highly inventive oath. Her lips twitched, surprising her. Her head tipped, her curiosity caught. The man was closer now. Pippa had told her that they had a new neighbor. Perhaps the stranger was he, Alexander Kane.

He was talking again. Something about a missing dog and his own stupidity for getting lost looking for the fool. Knowing she had waited too long to escape before he heard, if not saw, her, she held Mystic in place. With her light clothes and

Mystic's gray coloring to match the fog, the man might pass her without noticing if they stayed motionless.

Alex stumbled again, righting himself, and limped to a large boulder to sit down. He was surprisingly hot, irritated, and not in the mood to do any more looking. He would rest, then return home. Dog would find his way to the house eventually. He leaned back on his rocky perch, letting his eyes wander over the small clearing. Suddenly he caught a flicker of movement off to his right. His gaze sharpened hopefully.

"Dog," he called.

Lorelei sighed soundlessly at the tiny fidget that had drawn the man's attention. Whoever the stranger was, he was tall and slim. Hair with more red highlights than her own was tousled as though the owner had been in too much of a hurry to comb it. Some would have called him handsome, but that wasn't what held her interest. It was the leashed vitality radiating from him even as he sat on the boulder. She had the feeling that any second he would rush to his feet and take off on some precharted course, perhaps a risky one, and succeed where others would have failed. Intense. Driven. The words flitted through her mind and settled in as though they belonged to the man and her image of him. She sighed deeply without realizing it, and Mystic moved again. She stilled instantly, hoping he had not caught the second betraying motion. It would seem her luck was out, she realized as his head turned, his gaze seeming to pierce the mist to pin her in place. The stranger had sharp eyes, for Mystic had barely twitched.

The flicker came again, but no sign of his pet. Frowning, Alex tensed slightly. As far as he knew, there was nothing larger than a raccoon or two in the woods. "Is there someone there? Whoever or whatever you are, you might as well show yourself. From what little I can make out you have to be larger than I am," Alex said, his eyes becoming accustomed to looking through the fog on the edges of the clearing. Whatever was watching him, it was no 'coon, nor did he feel any threat. "I hope you're friendly, because I'll tell you the truth, I don't have a weapon to my name, and if I try running out of here, I'm more likely to fall over one of these roots. I wish you would show yourself. I'm basically harmless."

Lorelei was torn between responding to the coaxing quality of that voice and backing away. Oddly, she wanted to go forward more than she wanted to hide. Puzzled, intrigued at her own reactions, she didn't notice that she relaxed her grip on the reins. Mystic solved the problem for both her and Alex. He took two steps out of the mist.

Alex's eyes widened as a beautiful woman on a silver horse slipped into the clearing. "I know I'm awake so you can't be a dream," he murmured, staring at her. A dark braid flowed over one shoulder and breast to lie like a silken coil on her thigh. She was slender, her head and throat swathed in a brightly colored fabric that trailed down her back. Her hands were fragile on the reins, as still and calm as the pale eyes that looked at him as though they had never seen a man before. He rose. She stiffened, and the horse moved back a step.

Startled, Alex froze. "I won't hurt you," he said quietly, watching her closely. "I just bought the house on the hill. I'm new in town, which is why you don't know me. My name is Alexander Kane." He tried a faint smile, hoping to reassure her.

Needing to hide from that smile and the gentle voice, Lorelei looked in the direction that she knew his house lay. He really was lost. The fog would not burn off for hours yet. Unless she helped him he would be stuck in the thicket or wandering around for a long time.

Alex studied the woman, wondering why she didn't speak. She seemed to be thinking. "Are you lost like I am?" he asked, wanting her to look at him again. He didn't think he had ever seen one human being who could hold so still. The horse showed more motion, more life than she.

Lorelei shook her head slightly, turning just enough to see him out of the corners of her eyes.

Alex studied her, curious at her continued silence. The woman was incredibly shy. With each passing moment he found it more important that he get her to look at him fully, to answer. Moving carefully, he eased back onto the rock. "I lost my dog. I don't suppose you've seen a nondescript mongrel wandering around here, have you?"

Lorelei shook her head, relaxing slightly at the easy way he spoke.

Alex frowned slightly as she continued to gesture rather than speak. Suddenly an unexpected idea began to take hold. Maybe the woman wasn't just incredibly shy. Maybe she couldn't talk. A surge of anger and pain knifed through him at the thought. To be so beautiful and then to be denied the joy of words. He couldn't even begin to imagine what her life would be like.

Afraid of hurting her by asking, he made himself respond to her silence as though it were natural, for in a way it was. She fit the stillness of the woods and the fog. "All right, lovely lady from the mist. I have always loved a mystery. If I ask questions, will you answer with a nod or two?"

His question took her by surprise. Lorelei faced him fully, her brows arching curiously. The gentleness of his voice touched her. For a moment she wanted to try the vocal cords she knew from experience would fail her. Slowly, she nodded. His smile was beautiful to see, a sunrise after the darkest night. She bathed in it, warming places that had been cold. Her lips curved as she returned the warmth to the giver.

Alex wanted to reach out to her when he saw her smile. But for the first time in his life he knew fear. She was poised on the edge of escape. One move and he felt she would run, never to return. He frowned slightly at the thought, then wished he hadn't betrayed himself with the gesture, for the woman's smile died, her eyes sliding past his to the concealing shadows behind her.

"No, don't go. Please!" he pleaded swiftly. "Can't you stay?" In his haste to keep her with him he had almost forgotten to plan his words in a way that she could give a yes or no reply.

Lorelei only hesitated for a moment before nodding without looking at him. She didn't want to go. For the first time in a long while she wanted to be near someone other than her aunt. She didn't understand the feeling, but she could see no harm in giving into the urge.

"Do you live around here?"

She nodded again, turning her head slightly to watch him.

"I bought the old Duran place. Do you know it?"

She nodded.

"Could you lead me there?"

Another nod.

Alex smiled, feeling absurdly pleased that he could communicate with her. "Good." Now for the next step. Could he get close to her? Just a moment would do. Part of him knew she was real, but he had the strangest need to touch her, to feel her warmth for an instant. "Will the horse take us both, because I don't think I'm going to be able to keep you in sight unless I'm either hanging on to something or riding with you? The mist over my way is really thick.''

Lorelei shook her head, knowing that Mystic, for all his good manners where she was concerned, had no love of the male of the species on his back. Nor would he allow a stranger to hang onto his tack. The best way would be for her to get off and lead the stallion, but the roughness of the terrain combined with the early hour would make the morning stiffness in her leg even worse than usual. A faint breeze stirred the trees, catching the edges of her scarf. One hand crept reflexively to her throat. Her shirt was a button-up. She could cover the scar even without the scarf. The silk was long and strong. It would make a good lead. Working quickly before she lost her nerve, she unwound the fabric and leaned over to slip one end under her foot where it rested in the stirrup. She didn't want to tie it for safety's sake.

Alex watched her, for a moment unsure what she had in mind. It was only as she guided the horse nearer so that the cloth trailed close enough for him to grab that he realized what she intended doing. Disappointment was swift, but he hid it. There was a fragile look about her that hadn't been apparent at first. He had the fleeting impression of a badly hurt creature, perhaps frightened even of the smallest human contact. She seemed relaxed on the horse but so wary of him he longed to tell her he wouldn't harm a hair on her beautiful head. Instead, because he did not understand what the problem was, he had no choice but to give her the space she seemed to need to feel comfortable.

"Not only beautiful but intelligent, too," he murmured, smiling slightly. He walked easily off to one side of the horse. The fabric in his hands was so light he felt as if he had hold of nothing. Her scent clung to it, teasing his senses as her silence teased his mind. "I don't know much about horses, but this one is a beauty. Is he yours?"

He glanced at her profile as she nodded. Even from the side she was exquisite. "Are we far from my place?" At her negative reply, he continued. "Will you come in for coffee? It's the least I can do after your rescue." Her refusal was more than disappointing. He walked in silence for a few moments, trying to think of a way to prolong their time together. The mist began to thicken around them. He looked ahead, seeing the trees thinning. Soon the fog would envelop them and he would not be able to see her face clearly. "I don't even know your name," he said softly, not intending for her to hear.

But Lorelei heard. The need to speak had never been greater. She had learned to live without regrets with what the accident had done to—and for—her. Her name. Such a simple request, but one she could not fill with words. Her chin lifted, her eyes staring into the clouds of mist before her.

All she could feel of Alex now was his voice, and all he had of her was a length of silk in his hands. That was the way things had to stay, for to risk a closer acquaintance would mean baring her past and seeing the dreaded pity in his eyes or, worse yet, suffering either rejection or smothering concern. She had had enough of all three to last a lifetime. The shadows and silence were far better companions, more dependable, more kind, and more generous. Her heels touched Mystic's sides, increasing the pace slightly. The sooner she was free of Alex, the sooner she could forget they had met.

Alex felt the ground change and the horse speed up. He recognized the beginning of the path home. He could have found his way from here, but he hoped the woman would not know that. "Are we almost there?" For a moment he forgot she could no longer see him. Maybe if he played dumb she would stay longer. A foolish strategy perhaps, but he was willing to try anything to keep her near for a while longer.

The house loomed up all too swiftly out of the gloom. The second he saw the shape, the tension on the silk went slack. Alex pulled the fabric toward him, knowing even as he did that she was no longer beside him. "Lovely lady," he called, more lonely than he would have believed possible.

No sound answered back. No soft shadow joined him in the mist. She was gone. What the mist had given in silence, it had taken back in silence.

Alex lifted the silk to his lips, her scent surrounding him. Light, delicate, a hint of spice and flowers as unique in its fragrance as she was in her beauty. "Lovely lady, I thrive on challenges," he whispered to the fog. "I will find you."

He mounted the steps to his back door. The dog waited for him on the porch. He reached down, patting it. "Maybe you were a good impulse after all. Because of you I met a beauty without a name."

# TWO

Alex stared at the scarf hanging from the post of the old-fashioned bed he'd had custom made for his new home. He couldn't get the woman's image from his mind. Out of necessity, his life of late had not contained female companionship. The renovation of the house, the move from his apartment, plus the rearranging of his work and personal schedule to less stressful levels had taken a great deal of planning and implementation. He freely admitted he was lonely. The last four days had offered him free hours, instead of seconds, in which to realize that Brian had been more right than he knew about the direction his ambition was taking him. Even the women in his life, more often than not, were companions or business associates rather than lovers.

"Any man would have been affected by her," he assured himself, staring at the silk rainbow she had left behind. If he had not held it in his hands, he would have been certain his mind and the mist had created an exquisite illusion.

The phone rang, startling him out of his thoughts. He reached for it, his eyes still on the bright banner decorating his bed. The sound of his secretary's voice got his attention.

"I thought you said the caterers would be here by one," he said, feeling the relaxation leave his body. Tension tightened his muscles as he massaged the back of his neck. "They know I have thirty people coming for a housewarming at six tonight."

"That was the plan, but one of their trucks broke down. They're sending their chef and a two-man crew out now so they'll only be an hour late. I just wanted to let you know."

Alex sat down on the bed striving to hold on to his temper. Six months ago he might not have made the effort. "All right. I suppose the worse that can happen is that we all end up bunking down here to sleep off hangovers. I've already got the liquor cabinet stocked." He sighed deeply, forcing his muscles to unclench. If he intended to make this new life work he had to stop letting every little thing get to him.

His secretary laughed. "Boss, no one who knows you would believe you'd ever let yourself loose enough to get a hangover. I don't think I have ever seen you drunk or even mildly intoxicated. Besides, I think most of us will be too busy looking at the place that enticed you to give up the excitement of Atlanta for the rural pleasures of watching grass grow and frogs croak,'' she teased with the familiarity of a woman who had worked by his side since the day he had started his business on a wing, a prayer, and a whopping loan from the bank.

"Just make sure you don't get lost on the way,'' Alex warned, chuckling. "You might end up owning a retreat of your own.''

"Not on your life. Someone has to mind the store while you're out in the sticks communing with nature Saturday through Monday. Although, come to think of it, I'd better shut up. You get more work done in the four days left than most people get in ten. I think I like the idea of having the office to myself. Maybe I can stay even this way.'' Laughing, she hung up the phone.

"Lori, is that you?'' Pippa called from the kitchen.

"Who else?'' Lorelei asked in a stiltedly husky voice. She grimaced at the sound emerging from her throat. It had been nine years and she still couldn't get used to how she sounded in the morning. Once she was up and speaking for a couple of hours her speech improved, although it never lost the husky tones that were so different from her voice before the accident—and the piece of glass that had damaged her vocal cords.

Philippa, better known as Pippa to her friends and J.B. Starr to her sci-fi readers, leaned one hip against the counter and handed her niece a cup of coffee. "Your hair is wet," she observed.

"I know. It's foggy out."

"You usually wear a scarf."

"I lost it." Lorelei shrugged, a little surprised she withheld mentioning her encounter with their new neighbor. Pippa and she had a special relationship, one that included honesty, the right to privacy, and caring. In the years they had shared the same house, Lorelei had not felt the need to hide anything from her aunt. "In the trees. I didn't notice until I got home," she elaborated, trying to shake off a feeling of guilt.

Pippa studied her. "You know there is one thing a writer learns early on. It's how to read people. You, my dear, are spinning me a tale. I have to wonder why." She sipped her herbal tea, waiting but not pushing.

"I wish you were still in the middle of a book," Lorelei muttered on a sigh. Pippa had the tenacity of a bull dog when her curiosity was aroused.

Pippa laughed softly. "What you mean is, you wish I still had my head so deep in the plot of my gory aliens, as you call them, that I wouldn't know what my favorite relative was up to," she corrected bluntly.

"I met that man," Lorelei admitted, her confusion coloring her words.

Pippa's light-blond brows climbed at the tone. "What man?"

"The new neighbor."

"Oh, that one." Pippa eyed her niece shrewdly. "He's one sexy hunk. I've met him in town a couple of times. I liked him, even if he is younger than I am. If he were five years older, that smile of his could turn in my direction any time."

Lorelei blinked, startled at the comment. Pippa was a beautiful woman, and only thirty-eight. She enjoyed a wide social life and made no secret of her determination to stay single. Her reasoning was that a writer was the very devil to live with on a full-time basis. "You're kidding."

Pippa stared at her, a wicked grin touching her lips. "Why should I? Just because you've retreated from the human race doesn't mean that I have."

"I haven't retreated exactly. I like it here," Lorelei denied, her voice cracking slightly with the force of her irritation. "And I'm tired of you implying that I have. What is it with you lately?"

All humor left Pippa's expression as she put down her cup to give Lorelei her full attention. "Nine years ago you came home to me as a badly scarred child looking for a place to lick her wounds. I was glad to have you. I still am. I love you. But I never expected you to dig yourself in and not even stick your nose out of this town for a look at the world."

Much as she would have liked to, Lorelei couldn't deny the summation of her life to date.

"Life is to be lived, not endured. I know you've decided you're content. You have your computers and those computer games you design, plus more money than you'll ever spend, first from the accident settlement and then from your professional success. But that isn't enough. Or at least it shouldn't be. People need people. You can't keep telling yourself that you're deficient somehow just because your body is no longer perfect. The plastic surgery repaired almost all of the damage, and you know it—or you would if you would ever really look at yourself."

Lorelei turned away to take a chair at the table. Pippa's comments stung.

"Don't look like that." Pippa sat down beside Lorelei. "I hate waste. You know that. I want to see you happy, not vegetating in the woods because you think that is the only place you can exist. You're beautiful. There are men out there who will tell you so if you would let them."

Lorelei glared at her, her disillusionment plain. "I limp. I'm about as graceful as a three-legged elephant, and a bull frog sounds better than I do in the mornings," Lorelei burst out angrily. "You know I tried to get back into the swing of things. It didn't work. Even my own family hovers around me like amateur nurses mumbling about what I shouldn't do for fear I'll fail or, worse yet, get hurt again. I hate being wrapped in cotton and catered to like an invalid. You don't and never have treated me that way."

Pippa's blue eyes glowed with temper and compassion. "You were in between surgeries back then. All of us were worried, including me, and you were in a rage from pain and loss and weren't in the mood for any rational thinking. And besides, you gave it a try, as you put it, for all of three months. And your family, with the notable exception of your brother Jason, is nothing but a bunch of muscle-bound fanatics who think the world lives or dies in the search for physical perfection." Pippa propped her elbows on the table, returning Lorelei's glare. "You came here because you were running away from the media, your family, friends, teammates, and coaches. *Olympia hopeful cut down in the prime of her career. Gymnast loses chance for the gold.* The headlines were terrible and, with your family totally involved in the Olympic scene, impossible to ignore. The reporters hounded us all day and night. The phone never stopped ringing. Home was bedlam and the hospital was only marginally better.

"But the point is that part of your life is over. I know you've accepted that, even making a new career and life-style to replace what was lost. But it's not enough. You need people, too. Everyone does." She held up a hand when Lorelei would have interrupted. "I know you have been in and out of the hospital for the last seven years just repairing the damage to your legs and face that the truck caused when it crashed into your car. That's why I haven't pushed you before now. You needed time to really heal. I kept hoping you would start to mix a little, but you haven't. Did you even know that Alex is having a housewarming tonight and half my friends have been invited, myself included? I'm going. And had you shown the least interest in getting out I would have wrangled an invitation for you as well.''

Lorelei stared at her hands to avoid facing Pippa's too-knowing eyes. Everything her aunt had said was the truth. She didn't want to go out anymore. "I hate the pity," she admitted roughly. "I hate the way I sound and I hate the limp.''

"And I hate self-pity."

Lorelei's head came up with a snap, her eyes kindling. "That's not fair.''

"Isn't it? You could have been in a wheelchair, and would have been if it hadn't been for your determination to prove the doctors wrong. I was, and am, proud of you for what you've done. That's why it hurts me to see you hiding out. Most of your scars are gone and, with the exception of your leg, those that remain barely show. And your voice isn't so terrible. In fact, except for the early part of the day, it's very sexy, a bedroom voice in fact. As for your limp, it's there, but your carriage and grace are there, too, and let me tell you they outweigh it by a country mile." Pippa banged her clenched hand on the table to emphasize her point.

Lorelei rose and walked stiffly to the sink to gaze out the window. "I'm afraid," she admitted finally, the secret something she had carried inside since the first moment that she realized everyone she cared about was treating her as a cripple. "My own family couldn't handle what happened to me, and they tried."

"Fiddle. Your whole fmaily thinks the only thing important in life is how physically fit a person is. The four of them between them wouldn't know a computer from a microwave without an instruction book. Besides you, Jason is the only one with a college education, and he didn't do it in between operations and half the time flat on his back. I love my sister, but if she has a brain it's in her bust size and her ability to excel in athletics. And your father isn't much better. It's a wonder to me that they could even produce a child with your IQ."

The dry bite of Pippa's tone tugged at Lorelei's sense of humor to displace some of her irritation. Even when Pippa was angry she had a way with words. "They're not that bad."

"Tell it to the man who has to balance their checkbook every month. The guy should get combat pay." Pippa got to her feet and joined Lorelei at the window. "It's not too late. Let me call Alex and get you an invitation."

"I can't." On seeing Pippa's disappointment, not to mention the crusading glint in her eye, Lorelei added, "I will think about all that you have said." She tried a smile, her voice coming easier with every word she spoke. "Besides, I wouldn't want to cramp your style with the bachelors of the neighborhood."

Pippa laughed throatily, for a moment more beautiful woman than unmarried aunt. The negligee she wore was as daring as it was elegant. The rich rose shade set off the white-blond of her hair and the long lines of a surprisingly lush figure, considering that she took after all the women in her family whose slenderness and height were the most dominant features of their genetic pool.

"You won't. Besides, I told you . . . the only one around here who is interesting is Alexander Kane and I'm not into younger men. Not to mention that he, like you, messes with computers. If I didn't have to use the hi-tech marvels, believe me I would settle for pen and paper or typewriter any day."

Lorelei laughed at Pippa's disgruntled expression. "Pet is a very nice machine. She hardly ever breaks down," she murmured teasingly.

Pippa picked up the skillet from the counter and moved to the stove. "Only since you did whatever magic you did with her innards. Before that, I was ready to tear my hair out," she muttered, her eyes narrowed in remembered frustration. "Stupid thing has eaten more of my best chapters than my worst editor," she added darkly.

Lorelei opened the refrigerator to pull out a carton of eggs. "It looks like this morning is a scrambled-egg morning."

Pippa broke three into a bowl. "So I can't cook all that well. It saves dieting."

"It also adds to starvation—mine." Lorelei took the skillet, turning down the fire so that the butter wouldn't burn in the bottom until she could ready the eggs. "Sometimes I think the only reason you agreed to have me stay with you after thwarting everyone's decidedly blatant attempts at getting you married or otherwise paired off was to get someone to cook for you."

"The thought did cross my mind. But the truth of the matter was, I was between books when I heard about your problem."

Lorelei shot Pippa a look. "In other words, you were looking for something to occupy your mind while you took one of your breaks that usually has all the earmarks of a three-pack-a-day smoker trying to quit for a week."

Pippa set the table and poured the juice. "I'm not that bad," she protested half irritably.

"Says who?" Lorelei turned out creamy scrambled eggs onto warm plates.

Pippa tipped her head, her brow wrinkled in thought. "Well, maybe half that bad," she amended. "But you'll have to admit I do write stories that can keep a body awake at night."

"Everyone should have such a goal in life."

"Is this the woman who writes of the knights of old and princess in the tower electronic games?"

Lorelei shrugged as she took her place at the table. "What can I say? I like Walt Disney better than Stephen King. Fortunately, there is room for both of us."

"Amen to that." Pippa dug into her breakfast. "So tell me, what are you going to do tonight while I'm off to see the new man in town?"

"Read. Watch TV. Maybe even sneak a peak at the new manuscript."

"Bor-r-r-ing," Pippa drawled.

"Says you." Lorelei buttered a slice of toast. "Tell you what. We'll compare evenings when you get home. I might have just as much fun in my way as you do in yours."

For one moment she felt regret for the life she led. Then she pushed the feeling away. Even if she attended the party Alex was giving, there was no guarantee he would be that interested in her. The man had big city written all over him—high energy, restless movements. She couldn't live like that with or without her physical problems. She needed the peace of the country and the environment she had created for herself in order to work and be content. She doubted Alex ever worried about being content. He was probably one of those movers and shakers she had only read about.

Lorelei stared at the computer scene depicting her hero facing a winged dragon. His weapons were gone, his horse stolen, and the princess was in imminent danger of being enchanted to the point of marriage to the evil Lord of the Ebony Realm. The end was near. Hope was only a dream. The young peasant, her hero and really a prince without a kingdom, had to win to lift the veil of forgetfulness from his eyes and restore his kingdom from the lost regions of the Black Desert.

Frowning, Lorelei contemplated the scene. By this time of day she usually had more accomplished, she thought with a sigh. The graphics were good, the story adequate. The hero had no life and the female wimp he was risking life and limb to rescue would have bred wimps in real life if the two were to marry. She needed something more in her characters. Entertainment was all well and good, but she was fed up with cardboard figures flitting across the screen. She wanted life and action. Spice, thrills, fire and passion: Her mind flashed warning at the word. Passion! She was beginning to sound like Pippa. It was all that talk of getting out and mingling that was making her so disenchanted with the characters that had fired her imagination only a week before.

"Lorelei, are you working or taking a break?"

Pippa's voice was soft through the thickness of the closed door to Lorelei's workroom. "A break," Lorelei called back, getting to her feet to stretch. Checking the clock on the shelf to her right, she grimaced at the late hour. It was almost six.

Pippa came in, glanced at the computer scene for a moment. "Where is our intrepid hero now?"

"Nowhere." Lorelei surveyed her aunt's outfit with raised eyebrows. Since she was in no mood to discuss her stubborn game, she opted for more interesting subjects. "Are you sure this party you're going to is only a housewarming. From the looks of that purple pantsuit there is going to be more warming than anyone planned for. I thought you said Alex Kane was too young for you."

Pippa laughed as she looked down at herself. "But I didn't say he would be the only eligible male there. Besides about fifteen of the locals, he told me he's inviting an equal number of his Atlanta friends, at least three of whom are single and older than he is."

"You mean he offered you information like that on his guests without any prompting on your part? I don't believe it," Lorelei said skeptically.

"Maybe a teensy bit of prompting. Really very subtle if I do say so myself," Pippa returned complacently. "I had to have somewhere to wear this outfit after all."

The ensemble in question was an amethyst silk one-piece suit with a crossover bodice that draped lovingly over every rich curve of Pippa's figure. The fashion look was elegant sexuality blended with a hint of humor from the laughing flash of Pippa's eyes.

"It's a wonder you've escaped some lucky man's net until now," Lorelei murmured with a grin. "I pity the man you ever do single out. He won't stand a chance."

Pippa tossed her head, setting her pale hair shimmering in a tousled cloud against her shoulders. "My writing comes first. The male population has nothing to fear from me. I'm just out having a good time between books." She put an extra sway in her hips as she opened the door. "It keeps me fresh and the ideas flowing. You should try it."

Lorelei followed her into the hall. "And if you have a subtle bone in your body, it's hiding in your little finger," Lorelei returned with a flash of spirit that had all but been burned out of her by the trauma of the past. Pippa's sudden, secretive smile caught her attention just before her aunt started down the stairs. Lorelei hurried to keep up, for once forgetting her limp. "I don't trust that look. What are you up to?"

"What *could* I be up to?" Pippa asked innocently.

"A hell of a lot," Lorelei replied promptly, having no trouble remembering that Pippa in full swing was perfectly capable of reorganizing the world. Few people would be a match for her irreverent, totally, when she wanted something, unscrupulous relative. If Pippa knew the meaning of the word no, Lorelei hadn't seen any sign of it. Any obstacles in her way were only things to stand on while Pippa got what she wanted.

"What are you planning?"

"Nothing, Lori." Pippa patted her arm and swirled an extravagant black velvet cloak lined with cream satin over her shoulders to ward off the chill of the night. "You are my favorite and most loved relative. I would never do anything that would hurt you. Remember that."

Lorelei groaned. "The last time you said that to me you bought Mystic and dared me to prove the doctors wrong about my legs and my future mobility by riding him."

"It worked, didn't it?" Pippa's eyes were clear, bright, and, at the same time, unreadable. "You had the courage, you just needed someone to believe in you. Almost everyone else was too busy feeling sorry for you to be of any support."

Lorelei felt an unaccustomed sting of tears. The last time she had cried had been when the doctors told her her Olympic dream would never have a chance to become reality. Impulsively she hugged Pippa close. "Thanks for being there," she whispered before releasing her quickly and stepping back. "Now, get out of here before I drench your gorgeous self. Go dazzle some unwary male and let me get back to work on my bumbling hero."

# THREE

Alex saw Pippa Weldon arrive. Like every other male in the room his gaze slipped appreciatively over her silk-draped form. He moved to greet her, a little astounded at his almost academic interest in the sexiest woman, single or otherwise, at his party. "Are you alone?" he asked as he joined her.

Pippa shrugged, her skin shimmering like polished ivory in the subdued lighting. Alex noted the gesture without a trace of feeling. His lady of the mist had skin with the luster and satin smoothness of the finest pearls, though more touchable, warmer, infinitely more desirable. Her image rose for an instant, almost making him miss Pippa's response.

"I tried to unchain my niece from her precious computers, but she wouldn't let me."

A little annoyed at his lapse, he forced himself to concentrate. "I didn't know your niece dabbled in computers. With the grapevine in this town I know I would have remembered if someone had mentioned it to me. In fact, now that I think about it, if you hadn't told me you had a niece, I wouldn't even have heard about her. What is she, a recluse or something?" He asked the question more out of politeness than interest for the woman who had befriended him almost from the first moment he had set foot in town.

"Or something," Pippa agreed, tucking her arm in his. "But let's not talk about Lorelei. I'm just dying to meet those unattached males you promised me."

Alex allowed himself to be led into the throng of people already gathered in his living room, but his mind, once again, was on the woman who had come to him out of the fog. She could have easily been called Lorelei, for she had stirred his senses as the sirens of old were reputed to do. Suddenly he wondered if Pippa knew his unknown rescuer.

"I met a woman this morning . . ." he began as he edged her toward one of the few quiet spots in the room.

"Oh?" One pale brow raised as Pippa waited.

"I wonder if you know her?"

"How can I tell if you don't describe her?"

He inclined his head, accepting the rebuke. He, who usually had a glib tongue, was surprisingly awkward about discussing his lovely lady with anyone. "She's dark where you're fair, but her figure is much as yours. She rode a silver horse as though she were born to the saddle and she had the gift of silence and grace." He shifted uncomfortably on the last, not often given to poetic turns of phrase.

"You sound impressed by her. Attracted, perhaps?"

He looked into clear eyes, for an instant seeing no more than his own reflection. He frowned slightly, looking deeper as something about her tone demanded he look closer. "Maybe. I don't know her name." He should have known better than to discuss his chance encounter with Pippa. His experiences thus far with her had revealed a razor-sharp mind and a wicked sense of humor and mischief. Right now her eyes held a spark of unnerving laughter. He was sure of it.

"And if I told you?"

Feeling strangely irritated, he asked, "*Do* you know her?"

"I might."

He marked the vague response that didn't fit with the woman he had begun to know. Pippa was not a vague woman. Alex's curiosity deepened, his determination to get an answer firming. He hadn't gotten where he was in business without knowing when to push and when to play the waiting game.

"You haven't answered my question."

"That's because I don't have an answer."

Alex caught her arm when she started to move away. "Why?"

"One always values what one has to fight to attain."

"You don't strike me as a cryptic woman."

She smiled slightly. "I'm not. Actually I think I am rather a person who likes mazes and challenges and cabbages and kings." She touched his cheek. "And oddly, I rather like men like you who probably scare or intimidate half the female population." Laughing softly, she lifted her hand and glanced around the room, her eyes settling on a tall man standing alone near the bar set up in the corner for the occasion. "I think I see someone in need of rescuing," she murmured.

Alex followed her gaze. "Jonah will more likely send you on your way," he said, not expecting her to pay him any attention, which she didn't. Alex watched her weave her way through his guests, admiring her skill while feeling a surprising degree of irritation for her evasive tactics. She was up to something. He just couldn't think what—or why—she would involve him in any case.

Lorelei glared at the computer scene and redefined the word frustration. "You guys are giving me a royal pain in the posterior. *I* am your creator. You do not have my permission to lay about messing up my plans." Knowing she was wasting energy trying to get any more work finished, Lorelei backed up what she had done and punched out the computer.

She glanced at the clock as she left the room, surprised to find it was almost nine. Entering the kitchen to make a cup of tea, she wondered how Pippa was making out. A smile curved her lips at the thought of her aunt. She didn't need to wonder. She knew. Pippa had hold of life by the throat, and right now would be shaking it for all it was worth. Men would be around her like cold beings drawn to a flame and women would smile at her antics, for she never once took a man from his partner. Pippa played hard, but she played fair.

Lorelei looked out the window at the moon-silvered landscape. For the first time in her life she felt truly alone. Pippa had left her many times to go about her business, and Lorelei had always welcomed the silence. But not tonight. Suddenly an image floated into her mind to dispel the scene outside her home.

Alex. His dark eyes were tender, intent, her memory of his voice gentle, compelling in a way too alien to all she knew to be described. He made her feel things, funny little fluttery things that unsettled her. If she were honest, and she could be in her solitude, he was the reason she couldn't concentrate. He was the reason her hero seemed lifeless and dull.

Lorelei stirred restlessly. She wasn't tired, simply discouraged. She needed something to burn off the frustration that dulled her mind. She knew from experience a ride would help. With the moon out it would be easy to follow the lake path for a while. She wouldn't ride farther than the thicket, she decided as she went upstairs to exchange her shoes for riding boots and to collect a scarf. For a moment she regretted the loss of the one she had left with Alex. It was a favorite.

The air was crisp and cool when she let herself out the back door. It was so clear that the stars seemed to fall out of a black velvet sky to sprinkle the night with silver glitter. She saddled Mystic, crooning to the stallion as he stirred eagerly between her hands. He, too, liked the stillness of the night when all the world seemed empty but for them. Her movements were swift and sure as she swung into the saddle.

"Easy, boy," she whispered, bending low over his neck for a moment. "Soon we'll canter a bit, I promise."

Mystic stepped into the bit, his head tossing at the restraint. But he didn't pull hard. Lorelei laughed softly, enjoying his show of spirt. His muscles rippled beneath her as he cakewalked out of the yard.

"You hate being held down almost as much as I do," she said, letting out the reins a little. The stallion responded by sliding into a ground-eating trot. The breeze caressed Lorelei's face as she inhaled deeply, feeling the tension slip away. She eased her grip still more as the path leveled and smoothed and Mystic immediately replied with his rocking-chair canter. The thicket loomed ahead all too soon. Lorelei knew she should rein in but couldn't release the freedom of the ride. Tonight she needed the wind in her hair, the horse beneath her carrying her away from the confines of her life. She needed the freedom. Her eyes flashing with the reckless, dare-anything spirit that had once lifted her above the best of her gymnastic competitors, she guided Mystic through the trees at a far-from-sedate pace. The stallion snorted, changing leads with the agile grace of his kind. He came from a line of desert horses, trained for ground battles where man and horse had to be as one, able to turn and stop on a heartbeat.

The lake sparkled before them as they burst through the trees. Lorelei let him run for a moment longer before common sense held sway over the wildness flowing through her. Her scarf slipped from her unbound hair to trail like a bright pennant down her back. As she eased Mystic to a walk, she glanced to the house on the hill, hearing the music and the laughter of the party. The side-terrace doors were open, light spilling its golden warmth into the night. Drawn by the noise, the voices of the people she could not see, she moved closer, finally stopping on the edge of the grounds bordered by widely spaced oak trees.

Alex watched the party escalate around him. His housewarming was a success, the mix of people balanced and the food and drink plentiful. So

why wasn't he having a good time? Strangely
bored, he drifted toward the open terrace doors,
leaving the laughter and the gaiety behind. He
wouldn't be missed, he knew. His friends, old and
new, were enjoying getting acquainted with each
other.

The darkness closed around him as he leaned
against the porch railing staring toward the lake.
Who was she, the lovely lady without a voice?
And why wouldn't Pippa tell him about her? He
frowned thoughtfully. She had to live nearby, but
only his house and Pippa's lay in the area. Suddenly he swore at his own stupidity. No wonder
Pippa had demanded his intentions.

"Lorelei. Lorelei." The first was an exclama-
tion of surprise and discovery. The second almost
a verbal caress as he tasted the name that could
fit no other woman but his lady of the mist. He
glanced to the trees wondering what she was doing
now. Was she alone? Was she thinking of him?
A flicker of movement to his left caught his eye.
He focused on the large tree and the strange
shadow beside it. The movement came again. It
was Lorelei.

Excitement chased his boredom away. His hands
tightened on the railing. Obviously she didn't wish
to be seen. He didn't dare approach her directly,
for she might leave before he could reach her. He
stared at the grounds, searching for a path to catch
her unaware. The moment he found it, he turned
back inside. He would have to go out the front

and work his way around. Leaving the party in full swing, he ducked into the kitchen, on impulse snagging an unopened bottle of champagne and two glasses. Maybe he was crazy or touched with moon madness, but he had to see her again.

Lorelei sighed deeply as she watched Alex go back into the house. For a moment she had thought he had seen her. Every instinct had demanded she run, but she had been unable to turn away. Something about Alex called to her. She didn't understand herself, and that was new. Before the accident her only goal and focus had been attaining the perfection of mind, body, and skill to take her to the top of the gymnastics field. School and home life, in the normal sense of the word, ordinary childhood games and activities, dating, boys growing into men and girls growing into women and friendships of both sexes had been given up as she had prepared to realize her dream of the Olympic gold. Then the accident, the terrible ending of that dream. She had come to Pippa so empty of any experience but athletic training that she had felt far younger than her seventeen years. The months that had become years spent in and out of reconstructive surgery had still allowed for no growth as a woman. She had been too busy fighting for survival and quality of life for it to matter. In fact, she had not thought of her circumstances at all until Pippa had started to urge her to go out, to enter a world in which she had almost no experience. Even without her scars, her husky voice, and her limp she would have been at a disadvantage. Now she was hopelessly outclassed. She sighed deeply as she started to turn Mystic back the way they had come.

"Don't go."

Startled at the sound of the voice that had haunted her all day, Lorelei swung around, her hair belling out to dislodge the scarf. The silk slithered down her back before she could catch it. The moonlight fell fully on her face, painting silvered shadows on the ivory skin.

"I came a long way to share the night with you, Lorelei," he said softly as he stepped from the shadow of the large tree. "Can't you stay for a while?" he asked, moving closer, his eyes on hers.

Lorelei felt the impact of his gaze all the way to her toes. No one had ever looked at her in such a way. Intense, hungry almost, his eyes seemed to slide over her leaving a trail of fire in their wake. "You know my name," she whispered.

Surprised at the sound of her voice, Alex froze, her beauty suddenly taking secondary importance. "You can speak," he said in amazement. Where there had been curiosity, intrigue in mystery, there was a sense of betrayal and tarnishing of something special. "Were you just pretending to be mute this morning? Why?" The surge of disappointment was sharp and too intense for the occasion. He felt the fool for the feeling. Was it possible he would rather she be mute than playing some strange kind of trick?

The accusation stung, setting a small flame to her temper. Lorelei protested before she thought. "It was no trick," she denied forcefully. "I have trouble speaking clearly in the mornings so I don't speak until my throat loosens up." Her eyes widened in shock at what she had just said. No one, outside of her family, doctors, and Pippa knew about her voice. Needing to escape, Lorelei's hands tightened on the reins. Guessing her intentions, Alex stepped forward and grabbed the bridle near the bit. Startled at the stranger hanging on to his tack, Mystic reared with a snort of outrage. Alex was dragged off his feet and Lorelei was thrown off balance. Half in the saddle, she fought the horse, afraid that Alex would be hit by one of the stallion's hooves.

"Let go," she commanded, feeling the pain knife through her weak left leg.

"Like hell," he returned grimly, hanging on with all his strength. What Alex didn't know about horses he made up in determination to win the contest of power. Planting his feet, he pulled Mystic's head down, mumbling what he hoped was soothing horse talk.

Lorelei felt all four of Mystic's hooves touch ground. Shortening the reins, she kept the horse's head tight to his chest so that he couldn't rear again. Her arms ached with the strain, but she hardly noticed. She was in real trouble now with her leg. Every muscle tensed with pain and effort to take up the strain on her injured limb. Getting home would be a long, slow walk back.

Alex stared up at Lorelei, noticing first the drawn lines about her mouth and then the paleness of her face. ''If this horse frightens you so much, why do you ride him?'' he asked, misinterpreting.

''I am not frightened. Don't you know pain when you see it?'' The snappy return was a product of her days under the tutelage of demanding coaches, a defense mechanism for which she had thought she had outgrown the need.

''Where did you hurt yourself?'' Alex demanded, going from irritation to worry in an instant. ''Get down off this monster and I'll take you to the house. My friend Brian is up there, and he's a doctor.''

Appalled at the situation her impulse and uncharacteristic unruly tongue had gotten her into, Lorelei didn't temper her words. ''I will not get down.'' She had spent too many years surrounded by people who thought they knew what was good for her telling her what to do. She could no longer tolerate being commanded in any form.

Alex was accustomed to getting his own way. Lorelei's challenge was a red flag to an already irritated and unsettled bull. Freeing one hand, he slipped his arm around her waist and pulled her from the saddle into his arms. Mystic laid back his ears, fighting them both. Lorelei lost her grip on the reins as she felt herself falling. Alex released Mystic completely to catch her. If he had had less strength and balance, both would have landed in a heap on the unforgiving ground. As it was, Alex staggered back a few steps, ending up leaning against a tree with Lorelei pressed tight against his chest. His heart was beating fast, hers even faster as they froze in the shadows. He stared down at the pale oval of her face, hardly hearing Mystic take flight down the path toward home.

"If you were mine I would forbid you to ride that horse," he breathed, anger and concern mixed.

"Then it is fortunate that I belong to myself, isn't it," she returned promptly, a confusion of emotion making her voice crack. The sound embarrassed her. She glanced away, finding the act harder than it should have been. Swallowing, she willed herself to relax her throat before she made the situation worse. "Besides, it was your fault. You startled Mystic. He is very gentle with me as a rule. Had you not interfered, I would have been fine."

Alex stared at her, hardly able to believe his ears. "I just risked life and limb for you and that's the thanks I get?" he demanded incredulously. "I should have let you land on your a—rump on the ground."

Lorelei turned to glare at him. "Put me down. I was not in need of rescuing."

"And to think that I was worried about you."

Alex dropped the arm cradling her legs so that they thudded to the grass.

Lorelei whimpered as red-hot pain shot through her. Her arms slipped around Alex's neck and she clung to him as she fought the pain. Her mouth and face pressed against his chest, she missed his appalled expression and the way he took her weight, this time cradling her as something precious to be shielded with his body.

"Damn, I'm sorry, honey," he whispered next to her ear. "Take it easy. Relax if you can. Things always hurt worse when you tighten up like this. Hold on to me. I won't let you get hurt."

Lorelei slowed her breathing, listening to his words and obeying them. No one had ever held her this way. No one had helped her fight the pain, the muscle cramps, the aloneness that had become so much a part of her life. She had never leaned before, never trusted anyone enough to try. Had she been given a choice now, she wasn't sure she would have trusted Alex enough. Yet she *could* trust him, she realized with steadily increasing surprise. He was holding all her weight from what had to be a very uncomfortable position for him, but he hadn't moved a muscle. His hands were gentle on her back, but light enough not to hurt if he accidentally slid over the trouble spot. His voice was calm, soothing, as though he had all the time in the world to hold her.

She sighed deeply, letting the pain go and allowing his warmth to wrap around her. Her muscles, given relief from their extreme tension, trembled, showing the cost extracted in the weariness that was slowly invading her body.

"That's better. Lean on me, sweetheart. That's it. Can you tell me where the problem is?"

"My left leg. I have a bad knee. I twisted it when Mystic reared." She nestled her head under his chin, feeling oddly safe.

"I am going to take you to the house. Will it hurt if I lift you?"

Lorelei raised her head. "You can't . . . Your party. And besides, I'm too heavy to carry up that hill."

For the first time since he had found her that night, he smiled. "Honey, you're so light you almost feel like an illusion in my arms. Besides, I'll go slow. It isn't often I get to rescue a lovely lady in distress." He wanted her in his home and cared for by Brian. To get her there he suspected he would be better served if she were distracted, both physically and emotionally.

Startled at the light comment, she searched his eyes, seeking the truth. "Are you flirting with me?" she asked.

At her question, his gaze sharpened. She sounded genuinely curious. "I would think most men would flirt with you in this situation." He shifted her body so that he could slide his arm under her legs. "Why so surprised?" He felt the sudden tension in her body and frowned at it. "Why would you not think you're beautiful? You must know what you look like.''

"Yes, I know what I look like," she agreed flatly. She glanced around, needing to escape his eyes and the situation. "Damn, Mystic has taken off. How am I going to get home?''

"Your aunt will take you after Brian sees you.'' Tucking her strange reaction over her beauty to the back of his mind, Alex concentrated on getting her to help. "I'm going to pick you up and you're going to tell me the minute I hurt you, understand?''

"I won't see another doctor and I am not going to be carried into a room full of strangers staring at me,'' Lorelei protested in horror, turning back to him. "If you'll just get me to my aunt's car, I'll wait there until she's free.''

Alex was in no mood for an argument. "I think I liked you better when you didn't talk. At least then I wouldn't have to listen to such a load of nonsense. You're hurt and, according to you, it is my fault. I am taking you to the house. You are seeing a doctor if I have to sit on you while he examines you. And you are going to be carried up that hill, but not into a room full of strangers. In the first place they're all my friends and wouldn't stare. But more than that, I wouldn't do that to you. The last thing anyone wants when he or she is hurt are eyes following every move. I'm taking you in the back way to my room, and before you get any ideas, it's the only bedroom that I can guarantee won't have anyone in it, as some of my friends are staying the night. So shut that lovely mouth and lie back. Think of my carrying you as my penance for getting you hurt. Now tell me if you're comfortable.''

Without giving her a chance to come up with any more useless arguments, Alex bent carefully and took her weight in his arms. She stiffened, but didn't protest. He lifted her against his chest, waiting until he felt her soften against him. ''Now relax and think of how beautiful the night is.'' He started slowly up the hill.

Lorelei felt his muscles ripple with the effort, his arms strong and sure about her. Doing her best to distribute her weight to advantage for the trek, she stared at his profile. He was a handsome man, she realized in shock. She hadn't noticed that this morning. He smelled good, too—clean, male, with just a touch of cinnamon. The spicy scent appealed to her and matched the personality she was coming to associate with him.

''I'm sorry to be so much trouble,'' she murmured, knowing she owed him an apology. He was being kind and gentle.

Alex glanced down at her. That prim little voice with its bedroom huskiness was a marvel. He had been prepared for sulks or silence, not this curious kind of dignity. Lorelei was an intriguing mixture—innocent, quick to spit when angry, and just as quick to back down, independent and yet soft in his arms. "Honey, I have a feeling that you're apologizing for the wrong kind of trouble," he said with a grin. "You may even be apologizing to the wrong person."

# FOUR

The tingle of glass against glass, laughter and conversation drifted through the open windows as Alex carried Lorelei onto the porch toward his bedroom. They entered by the floor-to-ceiling windows that made up one wall. A light was on near the bed, casting a pool of gold over the mocha coverlet. Coffee au lait sheets were turned back as though ready for Alex to slip between. Lorelei glanced around the room. The walls were painted ivory, the furniture sleek yet giving the impression of an earlier era. A single portrait, a surrealistic rendition of woman rising from the sea, hung on the wall. Startled at the fantasy image in the sanctuary of a man she would have described as anything but given to legends and illusions, she studied the painting, hardly noticing that Alex had laid her down.

He straightened, his gaze following hers. "Officially it's titled *The First Woman*," he said musingly. "I used to call her 'Enchantress.' She was a gift from an artist I roomed with in college. She stays in every bedroom I have. She knows all my secrets." His eyes glinted with self-directed humor. "She's the perfect woman, always there, always beautiful, always silent, and never too busy to hear my troubles." He looked down at Lorelei. "Until this morning I didn't know she might have a real live sister."

Lorelei leaned back against the pillows, staring at him, unable to believe he meant what he was saying. "You don't even know me."

"I want to, but I have a feeling that you aren't prepared to believe me. I have to ask myself and you why."

Nervous and determined not to show it, Lorelei responded truthfully. "I don't get out much."

"Then I'll come to you." He eased onto the edge of the bed, being careful not to jar her. "I should be getting Brian for you right now, but I'm afraid to walk out that door for fear you'll leave. Talk to me, please."

Lorelei inhaled softly, tipped over the edge of nervousness into an unexpected excitement by the look in his eyes and the swift plea. "You go too fast," she protested, knowing she was playing with fire and yet wanting to feel the flames.

"And if I slow down?"

"I don't think it's in your nature to slow down."

"If I want something, I have more patience than you can possibly realize." He risked taking her hand, half expecting her to pull away. "Give me a chance unless you don't want to know me."

"That's not fair." He was almost forcing her into admitting that she found him appealing. She wasn't ready for that.

"I never offered to be fair, only patient."

Her temper stirred at the uncompromising reply. "If you call this patient, I'd like to know what you term impatience," she replied tartly, pulling her fingers from his. Immediately she missed his warmth and regretted her haste. "I am not the kind of woman you obviously expect." She knew even before he spoke that she regretted her hasty words. The warmth left his expression as his features tightened, his eyes darkening until no life flickered in the depths.

He tipped his head, the light touching the red highlights that lay trapped in the dark strands. "You have no idea what I expect."

Knowing she had to make him understand, she tried to explain. "You come from Atlanta. That isn't a city known for being kind to people. My aunt says you're in computers, hardware design. I know what kind of market and competition that involves. A dog fight is fairer. Obviously you're used to winning."

"I can't deny my history or what I am," Alex cut in, disturbed by her assessment but privately acknowledging its truth. What he couldn't and wouldn't acknowledge was her need to hold him at arm's length. "But that doesn't mean that I can't be more than you think you see."

His eyes were shrewd, seeing more than Lorelei wanted Alex to know. "Tell me why," she demanded, no longer able to ease around the situation.

"Why do I want to know you?"

She nodded without speaking.

He lifted his hand slowly, touching her cheek lightly. She shivered at the contact. Taking his fingers away, he showed her the fine quiver running through them. "That's why. It has never happened to me before. I looked up and saw you come out of the fog and I thought you were an illusion. When you didn't speak, I almost believed it. Then you dropped that . . ." He turned slightly to incline his head toward the silk scarf hanging from the bedpost. "I didn't feel or see an illusion. I saw a woman, more lovely than anyone I have ever known. A woman of silence, grace. A woman who stooped to help a man, a stranger, in trouble despite the fact that it was clear she wanted to walk away. I saw courage, and yet I felt such fear that I was puzzled then and now." He looked back at her. "Is it me?" he asked softly, almost hesitantly.

Lorelei inhaled slowly, carefully. She couldn't

answer him. She didn't want to know what he thought or felt. To know was somehow to have an obligation to the man. She could feel her muscles tightening in rejection of the idea. "There is no fear," she stated, lying, as she had never done in her life. "As for our meeting, that was nothing special. I could hear you cursing yards away. I even heard you talking about the dog. My aunt had told me we had a new neighbor, so again there was nothing special in running into you on that path. I will admit to not wanting to meet anyone face-to-face that early in the day. I already explained that my voice is not dependable then." She paused, fighting to make her tone as matter-of-fact as possible. "I'm still self-conscious enough not to want to make explanations if I can avoid it."

Alex studied her closely. "And that's it? No acknowledgment that you are as affected by me as I have admitted to being by you? You can pretend that I don't exist as a man?"

She shrugged, trying to shut her mind to the hurt and the anger shimmering below his calm surface. "I didn't say that."

"Then you will give us a chance to get to know each other?"

Lorelei searched his face, seeing the determination to have his way. Why not? His offer was simple despite the attraction between them. She felt a strange kind of loneliness in him, a kind of fellow feeling that she understood too well. "Perhaps,'' she said finally, her curiosity overriding her need to hold herself aloof.

His eyes lit, dark fire in the brandy depths. She hadn't given him all that he wanted, but she had allowed him a place to start. He leaned forward, caging her body with an arm on each side. His lips brushed hers once, lightly, testing for her response. When she didn't turn from him, he pressed more firmly. Her mouth softened beneath his but didn't open. Puzzled but not worried, he lightly traced the outline, silently asking for entrance. Her hands came up to his chest. He tensed as she made no move to deepen the kiss. Her fingers lingered on his shoulders, exploring almost hesitantly. Where his senses and relief had ruled, a faint whisper of curiosity made itself heard. While Lorelei wasn't repulsing him, neither was she participating in the kiss. It was almost as if she didn't know how. The thought was so startling that he drew back, forgetting her sore leg. His hasty move jarred her, making her groan. Instantly, concern replaced all other emotion.

"I'm a fool. I should have gotten Brian right away.'' He caught her hands in his, giving her strength while she fought the pain. "I'm sorry, honey. I didn't mean to hurt you.'' He waited until she opened her eyes. "Stay put. I'll be right back with some help.'' He lifted her fingers to his lips, kissing them before tucking them over her stomach and getting to his feet.

Lorelei stared after his retreating back, prey to

a dozen emotions, the physical discomfort of her injury not the most important. There in Alex's arms she had found something she hadn't known before. For a moment, she had wanted him to hold her closer, to touch more than her lips. Her fingers crept up to the smooth contours, tracing the path his tongue had taken. He had wanted her. The thought was warming and frightening at the same time. Before she had a chance to examine the idea further, Alex returned with a man almost as tall as he but not nearly as eye-catching. The introductions were dealt with speedily, and in no time Brian had gently examined her knee, asking questions about her accident and the treatment that had followed. The impersonality of his queries made it easy for Lorelei to answer, for she had become accustomed to the process of the long years of reconstructive surgery and physical therapy. When he was done with his exam, Brian pronounced her fit, with the exception of a slight muscle strain.

"I would say that you probably know your own body best, so I'll leave how you deal with this up to you. Just remember, it's important not to strain those muscles. You've done a remarkable job getting yourself to this point. Don't blow it by overdoing." He smiled slightly as he got to his feet. "You know the prescription. Rest and gentle exercise when you feel ready."

Lorelei nodded. "Thank you for not fussing," she murmured.

"I have a feeling you've had too much of that

already. You looked as if you would like to wring Alex's neck when he brought me in here.''

Lorelei pushed herself to a more upright position in the bed. "I promised myself that I would stay away from doctors as much as possible after the last operation. It wasn't anything personal," she hastened to assure him, feeling foolish at allowing anyone to see what she felt.

"I can understand that." He took a small vial from his bag and shook out a single pill. He got a glass of water from the bathroom then returned to Lorelei. "You probably don't feel too inclined to pills any more than you do to doctors. But I think a mild pain capsule would make you a lot more comfortable, and unless you're into suffering . . ." His voice was as gentle as his smile as he awaited her decision.

Lorelei hesitated briefly, then held out her hand. She took the medication and then lay back on the pillows.

Brian closed his bag and prepared to leave. "Try to remind yourself that the worst is over now. Your doctors did a fine job, and you did an even better one. Now, I'd best let Alex know you're all right before he starts beating down the door. My friend isn't the most placid male in the world under most conditions.''

"Doctor . . ." Lorelei said quickly.

He turned, his smile flashing. "You don't really need to call me that. You can try Brian."

She ignored the offer with a faint, worried

smile. "You won't tell him about the accident, will you?"

His brows rose at the request. "No. My oath, remember? But, if I'm not being too nosy, why wouldn't you want him to know? I can assure you Alex isn't the type to be put off by a mark or two if that's what's worrying you."

Lorelei almost corrected him, surprised at herself for even considering the idea. "Not everyone feels that way," she said slowly.

"You can count Alex out of that crowd," he stated definitely as he opened the door.

"Well, how is she?" Alex demanded, staring at Lorelei as he asked the question.

Brian laughed, glancing back over his shoulder. "See, I told you." He looked back at Alex. "Nothing's wrong with her that a little rest and careful exercise won't cure."

"Lori, darling." Pippa swept past both men as though they weren't there to settle gracefully beside her niece on the bed. She scanned Lorelei's face, satisfied with the color and relative absence of deep physical pain. "Riding about in the dark again, were you? I always knew you had all the courage in the family. You wouldn't catch me on that horse, moon or no moon."

Lorelei grinned at her aunt. "You're a terrible liar. Who was it who taught me to ride to begin with and then took me out for my first starlight ride?"

Alex stared at the madcap older woman, surprised at the need to give her a piece of his mind for exposing Lorelei to the risk of night-riding when she was clearly impaired to some degree. He might not know much about horses, but only a fool would miss the added danger of shadowed terrain and the creatures that prowled the land who might startle a horse enough to toss a rider.

Pippa shrugged slightly, a mischievous grin taking years from her age. "But, darling, I was trying to get you to like horses so that I wouldn't have to exercise mine every day."

"I would have thought you wouldn't have wanted your niece to risk her health this way," Alex muttered, unable to keep silent. Pippa seemed to be taking Lorelei's almost-fall too lightly. He joined the two women. "If I hadn't been there she might have been seriously hurt."

Pippa glanced at him in surprise, his pale brows winging upward. Before she could speak, Lorelei said, "I don't need a keeper."

Alex gave her an expressive look that took in her supine form and Brian's lingering presence. Lorelei returned the look in full measure, not prepared to allow him to coddle her.

"You could have fooled me."

"If it hadn't been for you in the first place, Mystic wouldn't have reared and I wouldn't have twisted my knee."

"This time, maybe. But if it had happened and you had been alone, you could still be out there in those woods by yourself for who knows how long. The ground gets wet and damp, the nights cold.''

Lorelei flushed at the biting tone, her temper rising despite the feeling of drowsiness that was stealing over her from the medication. She turned to her aunt. ''I hate to ask, Pippa, but could we go home? Now?''

Pippa rose, her lips twitching. ''We can, darling, but I must tell you that if your intention is to leave this very irritated man here, I'm afraid you're out of luck. He is driving you home in his car and carrying you upstairs to bed unless your doctor says you may walk, which I doubt.'' She looked at Brian.

He shook his head, his eyes twinkling.

''Don't say a word,'' Alex warned, seeing the storm signals in Lorelei's eyes. ''I am doing all of that, and you will behave yourself so that half the neighborhood won't know what happened.''

She glared up at him, caught by her own need of privacy. He had used the one argument guaranteed to get her cooperation, but she couldn't think how he had discovered the trick.

''I'll follow in my car.'' Pippa headed for the door.

''I'll keep the crowd downstairs happy until you return,'' Brian added before trailing Pippa out.

Lorelei and Alex were left alone, neither looking too happy about the situation. Alex closed the distance to the bed and bent down until his eyes were level with Lorelei's. ''I want you to tell me if I hurt you. With or without your cooperation, I'm taking you home.''

She searched his face, looking for the softness that she had glimpsed earlier. The harsh angles and planes were vaguely frightening, as was the tone of his voice. ''I've made you angry. Why?''

Her question pulled him up short. For a moment he thought she was kidding. Then the curious, probing look in her eyes got through to him. She really didn't understand. The memory of her lips, soft yet closed against him, returned. What was it about this woman that made him think of innocence. The body of a woman lay before him, but the clarity of her gaze held none of the worldliness or awareness that he was accustomed to. Without thinking about it, he had put her age in the late twenties. Now he wondered if he hadn't erred and erred badly.

''How old are you?'' he asked bluntly. He watched those pale eyes blink in surprise. When a frown touched her brow, it was all he could do not to reach out to smooth it away.

''Almost twenty-seven. How old did you think I was?''

Alex shook his head to clear it. Something about her didn't add up. Maybe it was the night or the way they had met that was making him imagine things that were not there. He slipped his arms beneath her before answering, this time his voice softer, less irritated. ''About that actually.''

Lorelei automatically slipped her arms around

his neck and leaned her head against his shoulder. "How old are you?"

"Thirty-two tonight, but going on a hundred some days at work," he answered wryly.

Lorelei studied him gravely, her lips twitching. His mood switch pleased her. The last thing she wanted to do was fight with him. "You don't look it." The tension slipped from her body as the medication began to take full effect. Her lashes drooped as she leaned into him.

He glanced down at her as he walked out onto the porch. "You don't think so?" One dark brow kicked up. "That's reassuring. I like to think I'm aging well."

"Like wine," she murmured, relaxing in the safety and sureness of his arms. Her eyes drifted shut. "You hold me so much more gently than the others."

"Others? What others?" Alex mumbled to himself as he paced the bedroom. He couldn't sleep although it was late and he was tired. All he could think about were Lorelei's last words before she had fallen into a light doze. She had looked so vulnerable in his arms that he had tried not to disturb her as he had settled her into the car and followed Pippa home. Lorelei had barely been awake when he had carried her up the stairs to her room to lay her on the bed. He had stayed only long enough to make sure Pippa didn't need him to help with getting her settled for the night before he had left.

What was it about Lorelei that made him worry so? She was fragile in appearance and yet she handled a stallion with consummate ease. Innocence. Vulnerability. The words kept cropping up in his mind. Her age defeated him. Baffled, more curious than ever, he laid his plans for getting to know her. Tomorrow, after his friends left . . . He stopped, suddenly remembering something that should have occurred to him before. Brian would have had to ask Lorelei questions in order to treat her. Forgetting the hour, he stalked from his room to the door at the end of the hall. He didn't knock, for he had no desire to awaken the rest of his guests.

"Brian, wake up. I need to talk to you."

Brian rolled over, peered at Alex in the darkness, and swore. "Is there something wrong?" he demanded sleepily as he got out of bed. "Someone sick?"

"No, nothing like that. I need to talk to you about Lorelei." Alex dropped into the chair near the bed. "I need to know about her."

Brian flopped back on the bed, reached for the lamp, and switched it on. "You woke me up in the middle of what's left of the night to quiz me on a woman who for all intents is a patient? Have you lost your mind? You know about doctor confidentiality."

"I don't want book, line, and verse of her medical history."

"I don't care what you want, I can't give it to you. Ask the lady. She didn't strike me as the kind of woman to hide behind tales and evasions. I found her straightforward and remarkably without guile."

"How old would you say she is?"

Brian stared at him in silence for a moment. "Actually I know her age, although I will admit she looks younger."

"And acts it?"

Brian frowned. "Just what are you getting at?"

"Doesn't she seem very . . ." Alex hesitated, searching for the proper word. "Naive?"

"No, I can't say that I found her so. She seemed remarkably clear-sighted to me. I certainly wouldn't want to pit my will against hers on anything I wanted. I think she would win."

It was Alex's turn to frown. "Meaning?"

Brian shook his head. "Again, I can't say any more. I'm sorry. Ask Lorelei. Besides, why all this interest? Is there something more in Tyrell than this house and the peace and calm being away from the pressures of the city is bringing to your life?"

"I don't know. I only met her this morning but she intrigues me. I don't mind admitting that I definitely intend to know her better. She baffles me, though." He paused, uncertain if he could confide in Brian without sounding as stupid as he felt. "I kissed her."

"Don't make it sound like such an unusual occurrence. You've been known to enjoy the ladies on occasion."

"That's just it. I do know something about women. The thing is, Lorelei doesn't seem to know anything about men. At least not about the mechanics of it. She's got the responses but not the technique."

"Did it ever occur to you that she might have been hurting too much to respond fully?"

Alex pounced on the possibility. "Was she?"

Brian sighed wearily. "No, I don't think so."

Alex considered the options. "You can't tell me, but I could tell you, couldn't I."

Brian knew where he was heading. "I still can't confirm your guesses."

"She told me about an accident. It left her voice impaired and her leg messed up."

"Hardly a medical description," Brian murmured.

"Something like that might take a while to heal, maybe even require extra surgeries and stuff." He watched Brian carefully, wishing his friend had less of a poker face.

"It could, but I'm not saying it did in this case."

"Could it take years?"

"If the accident was severe enough it could."

"Would there be scarring?"

"Depends."

"A woman, especially a woman just into adulthood, would be sensitive about that kind of thing. Perhaps sensitive enough to hide herself away in a little town."

"I never knew you had such an imagination," Brian remarked, neither agreeing nor disagreeing. "What's the point to all of this?"

"I need to know what I'm up against. If I knew her aunt better, I would even ask her rather than risk upsetting Lorelei with a bunch of questions."

Brian sat up in bed, staring at Alex. "Be careful, Alex. Even if half of what you suspect is true, and I'm not saying that it is, an affair with a woman with that kind of history and emotional trauma would be hard on both of you. And Tyrell is not Atlanta. People out here get married, not live together."

"I never said anything about either one."

"I know you. You don't do things half way. You wouldn't be worrying this problem like a starving dog with a single bone if you weren't more than mildly interested. When I told you to get in touch with the life you were leading, I didn't mean to go this far. Think of what you're doing. Give yourself a chance to settle down in this new place, find your feet. You're vulnerable right now."

Alex got to his feet, irritated at the warning. "I am not vulnerable. I'll admit I've been stupid about my work and the way I've been pushing myself. I'll even admit this move has been a lot more complicated and difficult to adjust to than I thought it would be, but I am not vulnerable. I *am* interested in Lorelei, but my only reason for wanting to know about her is because I don't want to inadvertently hurt her. She seems fragile, in need of care. I like her and I want to spend time with her. There is no long-range plan to seduce her rolling around in my head, and I promise you I don't have marriage on my mind. I've got enough to do to learn how to slow down." He headed for the door, annoyed and disappointed that Brian hadn't been more help.

Brian's mouth twitched at the disgruntled tone. "Anything you say, Alex."

Alex shot him a sharp look. "You're walking on thin ice, my friend."

Brian held up a hand. "I believe you're telling me the truth as you see it. I can't help it if I see something else."

"And I thought your profession made you good at reading people." He walked out, regretting the impulse that had sent him to Brian's room. He should have remembered his buddy, much as Lorelei's aunt, delighted in cryptic words. "Deliver me from obscure-sounding friends," he muttered on entering his bedroom. Now he had Brian positive he was setting up the beginnings of an affair. "Serves me right for being a blabbermouth." He flopped into bed and stared at the darkened ceiling. One thing about it, he had learned something. No way was he going to approach Pippa with any questions about Lorelei. Risk or not, he would direct his questions—and very carefully—to his lady of the mist herself.

# FIVE

Lorelei awoke late, stretching cautiously to test her leg. The faint discomfort was much less than she expected. She smiled slightly in relief before easing out of bed. After she showered, a few gentle exercises to loosen the muscles helped even more. Riding this morning would be pushing her luck, but she could work. She headed downstairs for breakfast, surprised to find Pippa at the stove.

"What are you doing in the kitchen this late? I would have thought you would be well into planning your next book my now," Lorelei said in greeting.

Pippa turned, looking her over carefully. "Actually, I was waiting for you. How are you feeling this morning?"

Lorelei grimaced ruefully. "Better than I deserve. Did Mystic get back all right last night?"

"He did. I unsaddled him and gave him a rub-down plus checked him to be sure he hadn't hurt himself on the way home. He's fine." Pippa moved to the oven to pull two plates of pancakes from the rack. "Juice is in the refrigerator and coffee in the pot."

Lorelei filled a cup before taking her seat. "You've been busy. To what do I owe the honor of your one and only culinary claim to fame?"

"It's a bribe."

Lorelei glanced up from her plate, her brows lifted. "For what?"

"Information. I'm dying of curiosity. How did you end up at Alex's?"

Lorelei poured honey onto her pancakes, trying to find an answer. "Would you believe an impulse that I should have ignored?"

"Why? I think it's great. Not about hurting yourself, but seeing Alex again."

"Pippa, you are beyond my comprehension. What could possibly be good about breaking up Alex's party, forcing him into a situation where he has to carry me all the way up the hill, and then to top that farce off, falling asleep in the car without even taking a minute to thank him for taking care of me? I feel like a first-class idiot."

"No one can fault you for nodding off from that pill Brian gave you. Besides, I doubt Alex would agree with you about that last point."

"Then I doubt the man's intelligence."

Pippa grinned. "I don't."

"With luck I won't see him again." She ignored the stab of disappointment her words brought.

"I'm betting that you do."

Pippa's tone would have been warning enough even without the Cheshire-cat smile that accompanied it. Lorelei stared at her aunt, a feeling of unease slipping over her. "What have you done?"

"Absolutely nothing," Pippa denied immediately. "I promise." She leaned forward to pat Lorelei's hand. "In this case I won't have to do a thing but sit back and watch."

"There won't be anything to watch."

Pippa's smile widened. "If you say so." She poured a generous amount of syrup onto her hotcakes and picked up her fork. "You'd better eat or your food will get cold," she added when Lorelei continued to stare at her.

"I hate that look. You get it every time you're plotting something, whether it's in one of your books or for real. I have never minded before—" She got no further, for Pippa interrupted.

"I have never hurt you, have I?" Pippa demanded, all signs of humor gone from her expression.

"No but . . ."

"I never meddle with people I don't care about. And so far my little plots have always turned out fine."

"There's always a first time."

"True. But, as I told you, in this case I don't think I'll have to do anything. I have a feeling nature is going to do just fine without my help."

It was unfortunate that Lorelei still remembered Pippa's words when she saw Alex's car pull into their drive. She had been at the computer all afternoon, stopping only for a light lunch. Her concentration had been spotty at best and her characters no more cooperative now than they had been the day before. As a consequence, she wasn't in the best frame of mind to greet her guest. But she made the effort. The alternative was leaving Alex in Pippa's Machiavellian hands when her aunt was clearly steering a course of high romance for her niece. Muttering dire threats at her best-loved relative's head, Lorelei hurried downstairs, arriving in the entrance hall at almost the same moment as Pippa.

"I thought you were working," the older woman murmured as Alex rang the bell.

"I was." Lorelei was a step ahead of Pippa to the door.

"I don't mind taking care of our visitor since you were so adamant about not seeing him again," Pippa offered with a glint in her eye.

"Oh, no," Lorelei retorted grimly, not trusting her aunt at all. With Pippa deciding that it was time she entered the world of man-woman relationships, there was no telling what she might do or say to her target of the hour, Alex Kane. "You were in your study the last time I looked, deep in the latest outline. You wouldn't have come down here if you didn't have something in mind.''

Pippa managed a wounded expression that would have won the hearts of the unwary, but Lorelei knew better than to be taken in. The doorbell pealed again.

"You don't trust me."

"I love you dearly, but your idea and mine of the truth are poles apart. Go back to your book. I'll see to Alex.''

Pippa glanced at the door as though being deprived of a threat, then shrugged resignedly. "All right, but I think you're being unfair.''

Lorelei waited only long enough to see Pippa disappear up the stairs before letting Alex in.

"I was beginning to think that neither of you were home,'' he said as he stepped into the hall.

Lorelei moved back, feeling crowded. The hassle with Pippa had driven all thoughts of her reactions to Alex from her mind. Now they returned full force to haunt her. Knowing she had to say something, Lorelei made a mental grab for composure and amnesia. "Pippa is working on her latest book and I was at the computer.''

Alex looked her over, taking in the way she was favoring her leg. "You're working?''

"It's not strenuous,'' she defended herself.

He frowned, then bent to sweep her into his arms before she could object. "You shouldn't be on that leg.''

Lorelei stiffened. "Put me down. You have no right."

"I'm taking the right as, according to you, I'm the one who let you get hurt in the first place." He started up the stairs.

Lorelei had enough presence of mind not to struggle on the steps, but the minute they reached the second-floor landing, she executed a simple gymnastic move and flipped out of his arms. Alex made a grab for her, thinking she was falling. Lorelei dodged, placing too much weight on her leg. Groaning, she staggered and would have gone down if Alex hadn't caught her. He swore roughly.

"What are you two up to out here?" Pippa demanded, opening the door of her study to peer out.

"I am trying to get away from a bully," Lorelei said through clenched teeth.

"So I see," Pippa murmured, observing the way Lorelei was leaning against Alex's chest. "An interesting way you have of going about it. I must try your technique sometime."

Alex's lips twitched at the droll tone and the irritated grunt from the woman he held in his arms. "Is she always so damn independent? I came over here expecting to find her in bed . . ."

"Now you are definitely a man after my own heart," Pippa said with a grin as she interrupted him. "I don't suppose you have an older brother with the same kind of direct mind?"

Alex blinked, staring at her in disbelief. "No,

I don't have a brother, older or otherwise," he replied finally, beginning to wonder if he shouldn't have stayed at home. All he had meant to do today was assure himself that Lorelei had sustained no lasting injury at his hands.

"Will you be quiet?" Lorelei demanded, glaring at her aunt. Her cheeks felt on fire, and she hadn't a hope that Alex wouldn't notice. There was nowhere to hide but in the chest pressed so close. "I swear you would embarrass the devil himself," she mumbled into Alex's shirt.

He glanced down at the dark head resting just above his heart. Without thinking, he stroked Lorelei's hair, sympathizing with her. "I know your aunt is outrageous. The whole town knows. I like it. I wish I had half as much fun with my own family."

"Well, I like that!" Pippa said.

Alex lifted his head, giving Pippa a stern look. He didn't bother to analyze the variety of emotions that chased across her face. All he wanted was her silence for Lorelei's sake. "I believe we interrupted your work," he prompted.

Pippa drew back into her study. "All right. I know when I am not wanted. If you're still here at dinner, you're invited," she added before shutting the door.

Alex noted the invitation but decided to reserve judgment until he could determine Lorelei's mood. He wanted to get to know her but he also didn't want someone else pushing her closer against her will. "I didn't mean to bully you," he murmured after a moment. "You worried me last night, and it was hell waiting until this afternoon to visit."

The almost apologetic tone touched Lorelei, soothing some of her embarrassment. Lifting her head caustiously, she searched his face. "I imagine your guests kept you busy."

He resisted the urge to tuck her head back against his chest where it felt as though it belonged. Instead he concentrated on their conversation and tried to tell his body that it was too soon to feel the hot burn of desire from the simple act of just holding a woman in his arms.

"They left before eight. Most of them have things to do this weekend." Unable to completely subdue all his needs, he lifted his fingers to her cheek, stroking lightly. "I didn't come because I hoped you would be resting, and I remembered what you said about your voice. I didn't want you feeling awkward because of me."

Lorelei looked into his eyes, surprised at the tenderness she found. His hands were light on her body, supporting and yet gentle. "It doesn't bother you?" she asked hesitantly. "It isn't very attractive."

"Your voice?"

She nodded.

There was a world of pain and disillusionment in her expression. Once again Alex felt as if he were sheltering someone very fragile, someone who had lost more than most could afford to give up. "You're so wrong. Your voice is different, I'll agree, but it's far from unattractive. In fact, if you want the truth, I find it compelling. It's husky, richer than a woman's usually is, and that little catch in it that occurs when you get emotional is damn arousing."

Lorelei stared at him, unable to believe he was serious. The comments of those who had thought she could not overhear them were as clear at that moment as they had been when spoken. No one, not even her family, had been comfortable with the sound of her speech. "I hate pity," she burst out, feeling strangely near to tears. For some reason she had not thought he would lie to her.

"Pity?" He drew her close, reading more in her face than he suspected she would have liked him to see. "It isn't pity." He moved his body gently against hers, letting her feel the response, which despite his best efforts at control, was taking over. "For what it's worth, it isn't flattery, either. I can't speak for the rest of the world, but for me it's the truth. You are one exquisite lady. That was my opinion when I thought you couldn't speak at all, and nothing has happened to make me change my mind. I never knew you before, and I have nothing to compare with, so don't get that in your little mind, either. It wouldn't matter even if I had known you before. Hell, I would think anyone who cared about you would have been so glad you survived that something as simple as a voice change and a slight limp wouldn't matter."

Despite her best efforts, his rough words unleashed the tears threatening to overflow. Liquid streams of grief over what was lost and relief over what had just been given marked her skin. Alex drew her head against his shoulder as he lifted her once again into his arms. Lorelei held him as though she would never let him go, not caring where he carried her as long as he held her in his arms.

Alex entered her bedroom, bypassing the bed to sit in the overstuffed chair near the window. He stared out at the landscape, stroking Lorelei's hair as she cried softly against him. Pain was a living thing in his arms. He ached to demand the answers to questions he had no right to ask. More than that, he wished he understood himself. It had been a long time since a woman had held any mystery for him. In his work, with his success, he had enjoyed a number of encounters, but he rarely had found a woman who held his interest long or who had appealed to him so immediately. Lorelei was the exception. He had a need to know everything about her. He wanted her in his arms and in his bed. But the moment he had kissed her, discovering that innocence that was so much a part of her, he had backed away. To build a relationship where both parties knew the rules was acceptable, but to take advantage of inexperience and vulnerability was completely out of the question. He had meant to keep his distance physically, if not emotionally—or at least that was what he had told himself on the way over. He had meant only to assure himself that Lorelei wasn't seriously injured because of him. He had ended up looking into those pale, clear eyes and knowing that all his fine words were just so much hogwash. The woman had him hooked and she didn't even know it.

Lorelei finally got control of herself. Her breath was jerky, but at least the tears had stopped. Where she was—on Alex's lap in her bedroom—and what she had allowed to happen in front of him was etched in her mind, making her mentally writhe in embarrassment.

"Better now?" Alex asked quietly.

She nodded.

Alex lifted her chin to survey her damp eyes. Reading the chagrin in them was easy. "I like holding you."

Her eyes widened. "Sure you do. You just love getting drenched or carrying me up hillsides because I'm too clumsy to stay on a horse," she muttered bitterly.

He laughed softly, shaking his head. She was so wary, so certain she was a burden. The people who had taught her the lies had a lot to answer for, and if there was any justice, one day Lorelei would recognize potential and hopefully show all her detractors just how wrong they were. "Actually I felt a bit like a hero last night. All strong and masculine helping a lady in distress. And today was interesting, too. I've never had a woman need me this way."

The tone was light, but the look in his eyes was anything but. Lorelei felt the warmth of his gaze slip into the cold, lonely places in her heart, thawing emotions she thought buried and others she hadn't known existed. The memory of his kiss rose. Her lips parted in an unconscious invitation at the thought.

Alex lowered his head slowly, not sure she meant the gesture but needing to take the chance. He wanted to have her taste on his lips again, to feel her soften in his arms one more time. Lorelei watched him come closer until she could see nothing but his face, his dark eyes. His mouth touched hers gently, brushing across her lips rather than taking them. Her mouth opened wider as she sought to deepen the contact, searching for more of the sweetness of his kiss. Alex's arms tightened on her body, pulling her closer, carefully probing her lips with his tongue, letting her feel his need but not demanding her response. The restraint was harder than anything he had ever done but worth it as she sighed against his mouth and began to imitate his movements.

The feel of her arms slipping around his neck and her soft groan of delight at his caresses nearly stole his control. Breathing hard, he eased back, cradling her against his shoulder. Her eyes were shut, her lashes dark fans on her cheeks. Her lips were red, faintly swollen, her breath coming in dainty pants that were almost unbearably arousing. He ached in places he hadn't remembered since he was an untried youth. He glanced at the bed so close and mentally damned his choice of rooms. The last thing he needed right now was more temptation. Lorelei was more than appealing. She was feminine dynamite cloaked in vulnerability.

"Honey, we had better move," Alex whispered roughly, resisting the urge to stroke her body. Her breasts were straining against the thin cotton of her blouse, the nipples like tiny points demanding his attention. He swallowed and tried to focus on something other than the lush feel of her in his arms. Even the thought of the IRS audit coming up in a few weeks did nothing to dull her power. "Lorelei, we have to move," he said desperately, getting to his feet with her in his arms.

Lorelei reluctantly opened her eyes, staring into Alex's face. "If you like," she murmured bemusedly. She touched his cheek, repeating the caress he had given her earlier. His flinch made her frown. "You don't like that? I did." She took her hand away, feeling strangely hurt.

Alex lowered her to her feet, keeping an arm around her waist. A sense of fair play only went so far. "I like it too much and you are in a very vulnerable position. I'm trying to remember that we barely know each other."

Lorelei blinked at the blunt honesty, the seductive haze rapidly disappearing from her mind. "I'm sorry," she apologized automatically, emotions tumbling so rapidly over themselves that she didn't know what she felt.

"I'm not." Alex thwarted her attempts to pull away completely. Good intentions be damned. He'd done his best. "I liked it and I very much would like to do more, now or in the future."

"I don't know," she said, hesitating. "We talked about this last night."

"And you never did answer me. Will you let me see you? Will you come out with me?" His first plan was better than walking away. At least it had a chance of success. Leaving Lorelei was impossible.

The first question was difficult enough to answer without the second. "Where?" she asked awkwardly.

Alex frowned at the tone more than the question. Was that fear he heard? he wondered, forgetting his needs as he considered hers. "What do you mean *where*? On a date. A picnic. A play. A restaurant."

Lorelei pushed out of his arms, turning toward the window. The fear returned, the humiliation of past trips to the outside world as vivid in the moment as they had been at the point of occurrence. People staring, reporters asking intrusive questions, whispers, the mute and sometimes not so mute sympathy. Shuddering at the images that were growing more real by the second she said abruptly, "I don't go out."

His brows rose at the uncompromising stance. "Ever? Why?"

"Look at me!" she commanded, turning fully

to face him. She spread her hands, indicating her damaged body. Couldn't he see what everyone else found so abhorrent.

He studied her, seeing her beauty, the purity of the eyes locked with his, the delicate form that moved so gracefully that one tended to overlook the limp that must pain her on occasion. "I'm looking, but I don't see anything to explain such a preposterous decision."

"I limp. I can't wear heels. I don't dance. Standing around at a party makes my leg hurt and I can't count on my voice to hold up. I hate people staring, asking questions, poking at my life."

Alex felt the bite of unreasoning, blind anger, finally getting a taste of the understanding he sought. Swearing mentally for the fools who had hurt her so completely, he closed the distance between them by a step. He leashed his anger, knowing it would not help her. "I don't care what anyone has ever said to you about your so-called deficiencies. I would be delighted to take you anywhere. As for what you physically don't feel up to, we'll find ways around those things or do other things instead. Do you think you're the only person who has to deny himself things? What do you think my moving to the country was all about? I had to have a change of life-style or risk an early death from a heart attack or stroke. And I was well on my way to an ulcer. I find the bonds of restriction chafing. I want to ride the highs of my business, not slow down to what I call a snail's pace. But I'm learning how to stop and breathe the air and see the sky. You're teaching me that, believe it or not. If I hadn't been out in the woods looking for that fool mutt of mine yesterday and if I hadn't sat on that rock with my eyes open to the world around me, I might not have even seen you." He reached out to catch her shoulders, his fingers caressing rather that imprisoning.

"I won't ask who hurt you, although I would give almost anything to know," he continued. "I want you to want to be with me, to share anything you like or nothing at all. Is that so very hard?"

Lorelei searched his eyes, seeing much more than she had expected and hints to so many things she didn't understand. The past was vivid, but not as bright as those brandy eyes that pleaded, demanded, and persuaded. She wanted to walk with him without wondering who was watching or what whispers lurked in the corners. She glanced around the room that had been her haven when she had needed one so badly and knew that her need was no longer the motivating force of her life. As Pippa had been trying to tell her, it was time she reentered the world.

"It is hard but not impossible," she murmured slowly, feeling her way. His smile was more than reward for the effort. She gathered her strength, knowing that if she were to do this, she had to be honest with Alex.

"You said you wanted to know about me . . ." she began, gazing intently into his eyes. His strength enfolded her, ready to be there if she needed to lean, but holding back until she called. The next words were easier for his supportive silence. "I was seventeen when my car got hit by a truck. I was on the way home from practice at the gym. I was in training for the pre-Olympics in gymnastics. The newspapers were touting me as a gold-medal contender. My coaches were over the moon with my progress, and I was positive I would pull off gold for America. I wanted it so badly. I worked twice as hard as the others. I *had* to be the best. Then the brakes failed on a truck and I was trapped in the wreckage of my car and my career. My hopes and dreams died in a shower of glass and blood." She touched her throat. "One of the largest slivers punctured my throat just deep enough to damage my vocal cords beyond repair." She shivered, reliving the feeling of confinement and helplessness. The need to stop remembering was growing but the need to share her past with Alex was still stronger.

"My kneecap was shattered, and one of the large bones was badly broken in two places. There were so many other injuries, internal mostly, which seemed to take forever to heal. The cuts on my face scarred, so I needed cosmetic surgery—and reconstructive surgery for the leg, some of which didn't work and had to be redone. In all, I've been in and out of the hospital for almost seven years. Even when I was out, I had to stay out of the sun until the skin grafts took."

Alex ached with every word Lorelei spoke, but he made himself hear every word. His admiration grew as her tale unfolded. "Is that the worst of it?" he asked gently when she paused.

She shook her head. "My father is a coach, my brothers are each team members of different sports, and my mother was a silver-medalist diver in her day." She tried to smile. "Our family has a tradition. But Jason, my older brother, and I were the stars, the gold-plated hope for individual golds in the Olympics. He had gotten only a silver four years before but was a sure bet for a gold this time. So I had family pressure to add to team and public pressure to make the gold-medal club."

Alex steeled himself against what he guessed was coming.

"I don't know if you can understand what being an Olympian means. Every moment, every muscle, every thought is straining for that perfection needed to excel, to beat all comers. Childhood is spent in training, relationships are irreparably altered. Some kids leave home to live with coaches or other families just to be near their trainers. I was lucky in that my father was the coach. I was unlucky in that he and my family saw me not as a daughter, sister, or person, but as a medalist-in-the-making. I gave up everything—willingly, it's true. I didn't date." She paused, thinking of the cost to those who had gone before her, failing because they had diverted their energies.

Alex found the answer to her innocence in the

simple statement of her growing-up years. She was an innocent in more ways than most women of the day.

"Those of us who did make outside friendships didn't have the consistency, the drive, the single-minded devotion it took to win. I wanted it so badly. Then the accident happened. I lay in that bed and listened to the doctors tell me I was lucky to survive despite the fact that all I had ever known was over. They explained my injuries, at one point trying to prepare me in case they couldn't repair my leg. When the operations were over, they told me to start a new life. I could walk, just barely. I didn't know anything but gymnastics, and the news people were like starving hounds at my heels. Everywhere I looked I saw pity and a mirror of all my flaws. The simplest athletic maneuver was impossible. I was flawed— broken as a doll smashed into a wall."

Her eyes were more silver than blue as she continued relentlessly. "First Jason came to me, touching me, for he rarely reaches out to anyone. He made me care just a little. Two days later Pippa arrived, breathing fire as only Pippa can. She swore at the nurses, snapped at my family, and sent the reporters away with a strip torn off every hide that came close enough for her to lay into. She made everyone mad, me most of all. She didn't sympathize or pat my hand with a pity-ing smile. She tossed the papers for Mystic and an airline ticket to Atlanta in my lap and demanded to know if I had had enough of wallowing in broken dreams. Was I ready to stand on my own or did I intend to be a cripple living off the insurance settlement for the rest of my life?''

This time a faint smile did work its way to her lips. ''I felt like throwing her out of my room. She knew it, too. She planted her hands on her hips and dared me to give it a shot.''

''I bet you did, too,'' Alex murmured, watching her.

Startled at his perception, Lorelei nodded. ''I tried. Almost fell flat on my face, too. Pippa caught me, sat me back down on the bed, and dared me to try again. It took three times before I decided I'd have to get well to get even. I took her ticket and the papers for the horse I didn't think I could ride—just to spite her, I told her. She just laughed and picked up my suitcase—to this day I'm not sure how or when she packed it—and walked out of the hospital with me trailing behind in a wheelchair that I hated. She brought me here. Stuck me on the second floor and told me if I expected to put my feet on Mother Earth again I had better get to work. She held my hand through every operation, listening to me fighting the pain and the frustration of healing. She bullied me, angered and challenged me. I learned to swear, and she learned to back off. By the time I mended enough to get even, I stopped wanting revenge and learned how much she had taught me about living. The only thing I couldn't do was leave here. I had been burned too badly, and until you came along even Pippa hadn't been able to get me to change my mind.''

# SIX

Alex studied Lorelei as she finished her tale. Her face was calm now, still, her body relaxed as though it had never known tension or pain. Whatever she had felt then had been transferred to him. He could understand her now. Her last words whispered into the far reaches of his mind, bringing a sweet burden and a sense of responsibility for someone other than himself. Suddenly, in trying to help her, he had solved part of the riddle of his own life. He had no one, and more than that he had not cared for anyone beyond himself. He cared now. He neither knew the depth that this one woman could draw from him nor was he afraid of finding out. He knew only that he would do anything to stay with her, give to her, and learn from her.

"I'm glad I can make you want to see the world again. I'm even more proud of you for wanting to try with that kind of a history," he said quietly. "Come with me. We'll take it slow and easy."

She almost smiled at the idea. "I haven't been around you enough to know you well, but I can tell you one thing—you don't know the meaning of slow or easy."

He couldn't deny the charge. "All my life I've had to fight for things—a college education, a start, a place in the marketplace, and to hold the spot I claimed for myself. My world has had one occupant—me, I'm ashamed to say. While you're venturing out again, I'm learning that I need people. I want you in my life, and I want a life to have you in. I need you to teach me how, for in spite of everything, you have succeeded in accomplishing what I could not do. You have created a new place for yourself and have been happy. Let me share what I am with you, and you share with me. Together I have a feeling we can climb any obstacle in front of us."

Alex wasn't completely sure what was prompting his words, but he had always gone by his instincts and been proven right too often not to trust them now. Lorelei's innocence aroused protective instincts he hadn't known he possessed, while her courage demanded his admiration. He wasn't sure that he could have put himself back together after a blow such as she had suffered, with or without the caring support of someone like

Pippa and the unknown Jason. He wanted to know this woman in a way that he had never experienced. He wanted to understand how she had rebuilt her life. He needed the qualities that she possessed—her clarity, her courage, her ability to accept her limitations and push through them without losing herself in the bargain—and maybe he could give her something in return. He could give her a buffer, a cushion as she tried her wings in the world she had left behind.

Lorelei wanted the freedom Alex was offering her. Just lately, she had begun to wonder about parties and plays, ball games and movies. She was no longer the person she had been, inhabiting the shadows of life. Alex was giving her an opportunity to expand her horizons without being alone when she tried. "You're sure?" she asked before she could lose her nerve.

"Yes."

"You'll tell me if you get tired of my snail's pace." The words were hard, but she had to say them.

"Yes." He spanned her waist with his hands but didn't draw her nearer, only held her securely. "As soon as you're recovered from that mess last night, we'll start. Tell me something you have always wanted to do."

"You'll think I'm crazy," she said after a moment, feeling a faint flicker of excitement for the future.

"Try me." He watched a tiny smile form on

her lips and stifled the need to taste it. Holding her was not the best idea, but his fingers seemed determined to sink into her warmth.

"I design video and computer games. I want to see them being used in a real setting like a video arcade. There isn't one in Tyrell, and the only one I know close by is always so crowded with people. The lines for some of the games are long. Pippa went in for me. Mine were the longest," Lorelei confessed in a rush.

Alex felt her longing and understood more than he suspected she realized. To perfect something in your mind and then be denied seeing it in a tangible form was perhaps the worst torture a creator could suffer. "I haven't been to an arcade in years. I like your choice very much but with one exception. Let's make it a lunch date," he suggested, thinking the place would be less crowded in the middle of the day and therefore put less of a strain on Lorelei. "What do you say we pick up a bucket of takeout chicken and have a picnic before we go?"

His hands slipped down to entwine with hers, threading her fingers through his. The desire that burned to slow boil within him at the simple gesture was more a curse than a blessing. "Virgin," his mind shouted in warning. His body ignored the word and went straight for the feeling. Her smile was pure witchery. Tension coiled tighter, his grip responding to the signal. He watched her eyes widen and darken as he lowered his head.

One kiss wouldn't hurt. People kissed all the time without anything happening, he assured himself, and he was a grown man capable of restraining his need until she was ready.

His lips took hers, gently when he would have rather plunged deep. Her soft groan whispered into his mouth as she leaned against him without restraint. The fire rose higher, flaring out of control before Alex knew what hit him. He molded her body to his, delighting in the way she flowed against him, her arms slipping around his neck and her breasts brushing his chest. She was all fire and sweetness in his arms and he couldn't get enough of the taste and feel of her. He had to touch her silken skin.

Lorelei responded to his need instinctively and with a passon that had lain dormant. His warmth and the relief of finding he still wanted to be near her after knowing her history were too much temptation to resist. "Teach me how to please you," she whispered against his lips as his hands curved around her breasts.

Alex froze at her words. He stared down at their tightly meshed bodies, at her nipples pouting eagerly in the cups of his palms, at the open blouse he didn't even remember unbuttoning. The door was open, and Pippa could have seen what he was doing. Desire drained away as self-directed anger took its place.

Lorelei lifted her eyes to his, suddenly aware of his stillness. "What's wrong?" she asked huskily.

Alex mentally reviewed every curse word he knew as he pulled her blouse together to cover the treasure he had no intention of seeking now. "*I* am, sweetheart." He worked up a smile to soften his withdrawal. "You are one lovely lady and I need a ice-cold shower and a brain transplant."

It took a second for his meaning to penetrate. When it did, Lorelei blushed faintly, embarrassment and dismay quick to douse her newly awakened emotions. "I didn't think." She tried to pull away, but he stopped her.

"Don't look like that," Alex commented, hating the way her eyes slid away from his. "You were beautiful. Everything any man would give his soul for."

She searched his eyes, needing the truth. She found it in the way he met her gaze. "But . . . ?"

Alex sighed deeply. "I want you. It's that simple. And I'm not going to let myself have you until I'm sure it's right for both of us. My life is a mess right now. Yours is in a state of change. We both need time, and I want to make sure we have that time. I don't want you hurt and I don't want to be hurt. You haven't known many men and I haven't known any virgins."

Where there had been fire, now there was ice. Lorelei pushed at his arms, struggling as she had not before. No one had ever spoken so bluntly to her before. Alex was taking the responsibility from her for what was happening between them. She might be inexperienced but she wasn't stupid.

"Let me get this straight. You think I would respond to any man the way I did to you?" Her brows rose as her voice softened. Because her heart instead of her head ruled her emotions, Lorelei missed the last part of Alex's confession.

"I didn't say you would—I said it could be that." Alex raked his fingers through his hair, for the first time wishing Lorelei were more like the women he was accustomed to.

"I'm a grown woman," she pointed out tartly. "You're not responsible for me."

His temper rose at her seemingly deliberate misunderstanding of his words. "You're a child in the big bad world. You haven't been exposed to the things most women cope with. By your own admission you haven't dated much either before the accident and certainly not after. You don't know anything, damn it! I can't take advantage of that!" he ended on a muted roar.

Lorelei stared at him, seeing that he believed what he was saying. Part of her wanted to argue he was wrong. The other half had to admit he was correct. She had almost no experience beyond a teen-age kiss or two and a couple of late-afternoon meetings at the hamburger takeout near the gym. He was trying to protect her from himself. "So what do we do?" she murmured after a moment.

"We go as planned, of course. Nothing is changed except I'm not as in control as I thought I was, so you'll have to help me be strong for both our sakes."

"How?"

Alex frowned as he considered the problem. His thoughts were interrupted as Pippa floated through the door, muttering weird-sounding words.

"If you had to die honorably and were given a choice, would you rather be given to the Urshca, god of silver life fluid, or Mecas, lord of fire night?"

Alex started at the question, unable to make sense of it. Lorelei forced her mind to her aunt's question, knowing she would stand there all day until she had an answer for the latest snag in her book. "Man or woman?"

"Both. Lovers. She's carrying his child, but he doesn't know that. The trayton does."

"What's a trayton?" Alex demanded, finding his interest caught, however unwillingly. Pippa looked more serious than he had ever seen her. Unless she got some answers, she was prepared to stand between Alex and Lorelei until Armageddon.

"Counsel of judges for the world of the Dancea. Lieta has taken to her bed a man of the fire world, a warrior known for his heart and courage. She has mated with him to fulfill the coming of the new age of her people. Her child is to rule the union of the warrior people, the Dancea, with the light race, of which Lieta is their guide."

Alex glanced at Lorelei, finding her staring at her aunt, obviously contemplating the intricacies of the unfolding plot.

"I assume the Dancea don't like this mating?" Alex guessed.

Pippa bestowed a smile that commended his intelligence. "But they are fair. They have given the couple a choice. It would be no contest really if Lieta weren't pregnant."

Alex and Lorelei frowned. "Why?" both asked at almost the same time.

"Lieta surrenders her powers of sight and transformation when she is with child. She is helpless until the birth. Andronika is more than mate—he is her survival and protector, all that stands between her and death." Pippa came farther into the room and flopped into the very chair in which Alex had held Lorelei, sharing the strength and comfort of his body as she had cried. "He must fight and win to save them both. But more than that, he must protect Lieta, for if she dies, he dies. His soul rests in her body to nourish the child they have made together. If he dies without it he roams the universe forever soulless." She focused on the pair. "So, tell me, how would you choose if you were weaponless and needing a chance, any chance, to survive with your woman and child? Drowning or incineration?"

Alex sighed deeply and took a seat on the end of the bed, his mind grappling with the tangled problem. "You're the writer. I would have thought you would know," he said when no clear answer presented itself.

Pippa looked surprised. Lorelei took the window seat, watching Alex and her aunt. "I never know where my characters are going. They lead, I follow. And sometimes they don't lead straight courses but rather leave clues. If I miss one, I could blow the scene, the chapter, or even the whole story."

"I don't see how either of them are going to get out of the mess you've woven around them," Alex commented. "The man has no weapons and apparently the woman, if she wasn't with child, has the only power available."

Pippa face lit up. "Not so. I shall give him the gift of reason, a voice to touch the gods." She hopped up, waving one hand in an abrupt good-bye as she went out muttering to herself.

Alex stared after her. "That's it?"

Lorelei smiled faintly. "Until the next time the plot takes off in a direction she hasn't planned on."

Alex shook his head. "What happens if she doesn't get an idea or an answer?" He should be leaving, but all he wanted to do was stay. It was quiet here, peaceful, now that the desire was tucked away. Lorelie's smile was gentle, easing the tension from his body.

"She badgers me until one of us gets a solution." Lorelei shifted carefully.

Alex caught the movement and frowned. "You should be in bed."

"You said that before."

He got to his feet but came no closer. "I'm

going now so you can rest. I'll call tomorrow, if that's all right?''

Lorelei started to get up. He stopped her with a gesture. ''If you want.''

Disappointment at her indifferent response surprised him with its intensity. ''I *do* want. We have a date, remember?''

''I remember,'' Lorelei murmured, watching him, recalling the feel of his arms about her, his mouth on hers.

He looked at her, seeing the memories in her eyes, and damned himself for a fool. One step brought him almost within touching distance until sanity prevailed. With a stifled oath, he turned and headed for the door. ''Stay off that leg,'' he commanded as he left.

''Has he called yet?'' Pippa asked, glancing up from her perusal of the afternoon paper.

Lorelei limped from the living-room window to the couch and sat down. ''No.''

''It's been two days.''

''I know.''

''And the weekend.''

''I know that, too.''

''You could call him.''

''We've had this discussion before. I won't call him. He said he would call and he will.'' Lorelei glared at Pippa and then pushed to her feet. ''I need a ride.''

Pippa turned the page as though her whole

attention was on the news. "When I went into town to church, I heard his housekeeper say he had to go into Atlanta for the weekend. Something about a contract problem."

Lorelei swung around, staring at her aunt. "You knew this all day and you didn't tell me?"

Pippa shrugged. "You didn't ask."

Lorelei clenched her hands into fists, stifling her temper. "Sometimes you could try the patience of a saint."

Pippa put down the paper and studied Lorelei. "If you need to talk, I'll listen."

The offer was tempting, but Lorelei resisted. "There isn't anything to talk about. I told Alex about the accident, my work, and my reasons for living the way I do." She almost smiled at the look of surprise on her aunt's face. "He suggested we go out together. I think he sort of sees me as a lame bird that needs someone to lean on."

"And you're going along with that image? Stunned would be putting my reaction mildly. I've spent the last year encouraging you to get out, but you've been adamant. And I can number on one hand the amount of people you've been this open with. Why him, if I may ask?"

Lorelei shrugged, uncomfortable with the question and having no real answer. "He was just there. It popped out. I can assure you I didn't plan it."

"I never thought you did. That would be my style, not yours. So now what?"

"I told you, we're going out. He doesn't seem to mind my leg or the fact I'm not capable of moving around like most people."

"Good for him. I knew the man had class."

Lorelei ignored her comment. Not wanting to get Pippa's matchmaking instincts aroused, Lorelei shaved the truth a bit. "But that's all there is."

"Everything has to start somewhere."

"What does that mean?" Lorelei demanded suspiciously, wondering if she had given herself away.

"Nothing. Just that I'm glad you're starting to move out of this little cocoon you've built here." Pippa opened her eyes wide, giving Lorelei her best innocent look. "What else could I mean?"

Lorelei sighed in exasperation. Pippa, despite evidence to the contrary, was a romantic. "I wish you would stop this insane notion of pairing us up. It's completely inappropriate. Alex is his own man and won't thank you for interfering in his life. And I know I can't take the pressure of wondering what you'll do next."

"So something did happen between you! Don't worry, honey, he'll come around." She picked up her paper, humming softly to herself.

Arguing with Pippa was like swimming up Niagara Falls, Lorelei decided. Impossible. The woman heard exactly what she wanted to hear and no more. But it wouldn't matter this time. Alex appeared strong enough to take on five Pippas and still come out on top. A faint smile touched her lips at the thought. Much as she loved her aunt, she would, just once, like to see her proven wrong.

Alex stared at the lights of his home as the car eased up the drive. Five days in the country had already given him a different perspective on city life. Even on the weekend, Atlanta had not been a comfortable place. It was crowded, the roads torn up as usual making travel a royal pain in the lower anatomy, and everything about the place shouted hurry up and wait. And the smog. Either it had been worse than usual or he was more sensitive to it. It had lain like a dingy haze over the city, dimming the sun and turning the air a reddish gray. He parked the car, got out, and took a deep breath, feeling freer and cleaner than he had since he had left Saturday afternoon. His impulse of buying this old place and fixing it up to live in was turning out to be a good idea. The quiet was still so thick it made him ache for street noise—not much but a little. And it did get a little lonely. Having a two-day-a-week housekeeper and a dog helped fill up the emptiness of having been surrounded by people for most of his life, but they weren't enough. Especially at moments like this. He was tired. It was early evening, and a solitary night stretched before him. He turned, glancing toward the lake.

Immediately, Lorelei's image filled his mind. Without thinking, he started down the path. She had been there waiting for him in his thoughts the whole weekend. Telling himself he had no business thinking about how lovely she was, how soft her lips were, how much he wanted her in his arms had done no good. His life was in a state of change. His business was booming, demanding all his time and attention even as he tried to eliminate some of the hours and stress involved. He simply didn't have the time to devote to a relationship nor did one fit into his plan at the moment. Up to now his women had been sexually aware and no more interested in a permanent commitment than he. He wanted to keep at least that part of his life untouched.

Lorelei, with her sudden passion and pale, smoldering eyes, was a threat to that course. If he had any sense he would walk away before he got them both hurt. Had she been less fragile, less sensitive to rejection because of her injuries, he might have been able to make the attempt. As it was, he was caught—caught by his need to help her embrace life again and his need to be near her, sharing the joy of discovery and bathing in the peace and stillness that seemed to surround her like an invisible cloak.

Sighing deeply, he stared at the lake stretched before him. "If you had a brain, Kane, you'd be dangerous," he muttered in resignation.

"I know the feeling," Lorelei said softly, urging Mystic closer.

Alex swung around, gazing at her as though he

had never seen her before. His memories hadn't done her justice. His mind knew it and his body was determined to reinforce the idea with a sharp pang of pleasure at the sight of her moving toward him. "Your leg must be better," he said, not really paying attention to his words.

She smiled slightly. "Almost back to normal, in fact. This is the first ride I've had." She studied him in the soft light of the setting sun. It was amazing, but the restlessness that had been plaguing her all weekend was gone. She felt at peace. "You look tired. Problems?"

Alex approached Mystic slowly, having learned the horse's idiosyncrasies from previous encounters. Other than a slight fidget which Lorelei easily controlled the stallion allowed Alex to place a hand on his neck. "I take it the town-crier system reported my departure?"

She laughed. "From your housekeeper to the entire congregation of Pippa's church. I heard about it today."

He shook his head, his lips twitching. "One of the hardest things to get used to around here is that everything I do seems to be of interest to people I don't even know. It took the work crews six months to get the house ready for me and I bet every thing that happened was reported as hourly news bulletins."

"Probably," she agreed.

Alex stared up at Lorelei, enjoying the feeling of having put a sparkle in her eyes and a humorous curve to her lips. His weariness slipped away, and with it the tension of the problem he had gone to Atlanta to solve. "I don't suppose you can cook," he murmured.

"Enough not to poison myself or starve."

"I can't. I'm hungry, and fool that I am, I told Mrs. Maple not to put anything out for me because I intended to stay in town."

She tipped her head, considering the situation. "Is this a polite way of asking me to make you a meal?"

"No, actually I think it is a blatant attempt to play on your sympathies." He wanted to be with her, but he needed a reason, something that wouldn't leave her feeling pressured and something that would occupy his too-vivid imagination. "Did it work?"

"As it happens, I haven't eaten, either." This time she glanced at his house.

"Please," he added, hoping she would refuse, wishing she wouldn't.

She looked back at him. "All right."

His eyes held hers as the hand lying on Mystic's neck slipped to her thigh, stroking the length lightly. He had to know even as he cursed himself for a fool for asking. "Did you miss me?"

Shivers of delight rippled over her at the touch of his hand. The warmth she had found in his arms was in the caress, heating the cold of loneliness from her body. "Yes," she whispered, unable to lie or evade his need to know. "More than I should have."

Her honesty shattered his resolution. Suddenly he found he couldn't keep to the course of noninvolvement he had chosen. He wanted her. Every look, every word, every gesture, told him that Lorelei wanted him with the same fiery need. He was fool to deny either of them. One day she would take a lover. Inexperienced or not, she had a right to decide who that lover would be. The thought freed him from his self-imposed restraint. Alex stepped closer so that his chest trapped her leg between him and the stallion. His hand moved higher, circling around her hips, feeling the woman-curve as though it had always known the contours. He felt her tremble in response even as he felt his own body tighten in arousal. Her scent was all around him, merging memories with the present. Nostrils flaring as he drank in the fragrance, he commanded abruptly, "Bend down."

Lorelei obeyed, her eyes holding his as she closed the distance between them. Their lips met, lightly at first, then with deeper intimacy, tongues entwining, sweetness and restrained need exploding between them. When Alex finally let her go, Lorelei was breathing deeply, her breasts heaving beneath the soft cotton shirt. Alex lifted his hands to her breasts, cupping the twin swells, soothing them with his touch as he looked into her eyes.

"I told myself I wouldn't do this. Hell, I promised myself I wouldn't do this. Make me stop."

For her sake he had to give her one more chance to deny him. He would gladly give her all the pleasure he knew to give, but he would not seduce her into his arms. She had to know what he offered.

"I can't," she replied, caught between an agony of wanting and the pleasure of his hands on her body.

"We're crazy, you and I."

"I don't care."

"You're sure?"

"For now."

"I don't want to hurt you. You deserve some happiness instead of pain."

"I don't know if anyone deserves either. We make what we want. Imperfect or complete, it is up to us."

Alex felt again the depth of her strength, admiring it even as he wished it were not there. Had it not been, she would have run from him and the danger he represented. As it was, she would stay. As would he. Fools? Gamblers? Winners? Only time would tell.

# SEVEN

"I thought you said you couldn't cook," Lorelei remarked, watching Alex toss the salad that would go with the mushroom, cheese, and ham omelet she was preparing.

He glanced up, grinning at her suspicious tone. "I don't. But even *I* can shred lettuce and chop green things into a bowl. Besides, after I shanghaied you into kitchen duty it was the least I could do." He left the salad, wiped his hands, and came to her. Cupping her face in his palms, he brushed her lips, smiling at her soft gasp of pleasure.

"What was that for?" She stared into his dark eyes, happier at that moment than she could ever remember being.

"For that funny little frown that you wear when you don't understand something and for coming with me and for saying yes." He dropped two more kisses on her lips, each deeper and more demanding than the last.

Lorelei slipped her arms around his waist, wanting him closer, wanting more of the delightful sensations that made her blood sing with life and her mind reel with joy. "I like the way you say thanks," she murmured against his mouth.

"You're not so bad yourself." He tipped her hips up so that she fit more closely to him. What Lorelei lacked in experience she made up for in willingness and generosity. Her every response was as clear and as pure as the honesty in her eyes. Without tricks, guile, or feminine illusions she enchanted and bewitched. It would have been easy to seduce her, for never having known passion she had no defense against its power. It was up to him to guide them safely through the sometimes rough, sometimes gentle storms of passion that awaited them. The responsibility was the heaviest, and the sweetest, burden he had known.

"This won't get supper done," she reminded him.

"No, but it sure makes a fantastic appetizer." He nuzzled her neck, deliberately tickling her. Her laughter was as spontaneous as her response to his touch. He drank in the sound as he teased her again. Her body writhed in his arms, inflaming his senses and straining his control. He accepted the torture for the joy of seeing her smile and watching her play.

"That's not fair," Lorelei gasped, struggling to free herself. "You're bigger than I am."

Mindful of the strain the game might put on her leg, he lifted her off her feet and set her on the counter behind her. "Almost anyone is bigger than you are. You could gain fifteen pounds and still look slender."

Lorelei pretended to pout, surprised at her enjoyment of Alex's teasing. Her life both before and after the accident had not allowed for nonsense and fun. "Is that a subtle way of telling me I'm a skinny beanpole?"

"That's a compliment, pretty lady. You're supposed to smile and say thank you," he returned, tasting her lips once, then nipping at her earlobe. "If you want to be extra nice you can even give me a compliment in return. Something along the lines of how sexy I am would be quite appropriate."

Lorelei wrapped her arms around him, giving in to the pleasure rippling through her. The warmth of his breath on her skin was highly erotic. Thinking of compliments for him and for the way he made her feel was so easy it was almost frightening. "You are very sexy," she purred, taking dead aim with a seductive tone. "Handsome. Your voice could melt an iceberg and I could wrap up in you on a cold night and be warm forever."

The rich sound of her voice, the words and the emotions that lent truth to what had started as a game slipped under Alex's guard, sending his libido into overdrive. He raised his head, his eyes level with hers, trying to remember that she was a virgin, that she had no conception of her feminine power. "Woman, you are going to get us both in trouble with that voice of yours. I said a *compliment*, not an invitation to the bedroom."

At his rough words the humor died out of the situation. In a flash, Lorelei tumbled from the dizzying heights of her own passion to the murky gray depths of humiliation and memories of the past. She didn't recognize the frustration driving him, only the sting of his rejection. She pulled her arms away as though his body were suddenly white-hot to the touch. "Let me down."

Alex caught her hips, stilling her attempts to retreat. The look on her face was more eloquent than any words. He silently cursed his quick tongue even as he tried to undo the damage. "Honey, I want you—quite a lot, to put it bluntly. I'm tired, it's late, and I'm trying to remember that you are new at this. I don't want you to do anything you'll regret and I don't want to do anything to you that will leave me hating myself in the morning."

Lorelei's hurt eased at the pleading yet commanding explanation. She raised her eyes to his, seeing the effort he was making for her sake. She touched his face, wondering at his continued understanding and gentleness when everything she had learned of him had warned her that he could be ruthless and that he didn't back off when he wanted something. "I haven't changed my mind," she murmured. Her fingers traced his lips. "I don't know much, but I want to learn . . . with you. But you'll have to tell me what to do, and how."

He shook his head before kissing her fingers, his tongue sliding down the length of her forefinger to her palm. He had tasted her honesty but found that he was still unprepared for her decision. With another woman he would have been in the bedroom right then. "You don't need teaching. Your instincts are as beautiful as you are. You make me want you too much." He smiled at her shocked look. "You don't believe me." He took her hand. Watching her carefully, ready to release her the moment she hesitated, he guided it to the heart of his desire. She neither pulled away nor hesitated. Instead, her eyes filled with curiosity, changing to delight as he nudged gently at her palm.

"I did that?" she whispered.

Alex felt her words slam into his being with the force of an explosion. No woman had ever shown him so clearly the reflection of his maleness. In this the teacher became the student.

Lorelei hardly noticed his expression. For so long she had thought of herself as flawed, crippled, incapable of attracting anything but pity and rejection in others. To find that a man of Alex's obvious sophistication could respond to her so completely opened the floodgates of her dammed-up emotions. Her fingers traced him, touching, kneading, feeling the heat beneath the cloth of his slacks. "Is this what the girls used to talk about? They never made it sound this exciting."

Alex bit back a groan as he covered her hand, pressing it hard against him. If he didn't stop her now he was going to embarrass both of them— no, make that *himself*. Considering how Lorelei was watching him, she would probably find his loss of control even more exciting. "I never knew virgins could be such a joy," he breathed, carrying her hand to his chest, trapping it there as he pulled her tight against him. Her body was pressed intimately against him, her every breath finding an echo in his.

"What do we do now?" Lorelei demanded, knowing no fear of the unexplored territory that lay before her. Alex had shown her that he would not rush her. She could feel his care with every touch and the way he watched her, gauging her reactions.

If ever there was a leading question, hers was it. Alex would have given his last dollar to lift her in his arms and carry her to his bed. But he was determined that Lorelei be completely comfortable with him. Their first time together would not be when he was tired and close to losing control. "*We* cook dinner and get our minds on something else besides how wildly enticing I find your body." He kissed her once, hard, his tongue probing deep in her mouth in an imitation of the way he would one day seek the heart of her heat and fire.

Lorelei met his lips hungrily, tasting, nipping gently as she copied the ways he had used to please her. Her hands stroked his chest, plucking at his nipples through the cloth of his shirt. His groan fired her need to a higher plane. She thrust against him, feeling tension gather in her body. She moaned in protest when he tore his mouth from hers. His breath was harsh, labored.

"Help me," he pleaded hoarsely. "I can't back off alone."

"But I don't want to back off. I want you."

He shut his eyes, pulling on strength he didn't know he had. "You have gotten your first real taste of passion. That's what you're wanting right now." He opened his eyes to stare at her, willing her to understand. "You are like a sleeping princess in those fairy tales mothers read to their children. You've just awakened and I am the man there with a kiss. I don't want this for us. Can't you see that? Sex, no matter how great, doesn't last. It doesn't leave you better than you were, it only assuages a momentary need. Give us a chance to know each other."

Lorelei searched his face as she listened. In her need of him, in her delight in finding that he wanted her, she had reached out like a child thoughtlessly grabbing for all the toys in the store. "I feel like a fool," Lorelei mumbled, dropping her lashes so that she wouldn't have to look at Alex.

He cupped her face in his palms. "Look at me, honey." He waited until she opened her eyes. "I love the way you respond to me. It's unbelievably special to see the way you feel, how I please you in your eyes. I like knowing you want to touch me, that you find me attractive. Any man would. So many women look at us as studs, satisfiers of a need, useful only because of the way we're built or how much money and power we have."

Lorelei heard the bitterness in Alex's voice. She felt something stir beneath the slowly fading desire. Sympathy, a strange kind of pain. "Someone hurt you," she guessed.

"No one special, but that is the way real life can be in my world. Not all scars are on the outside. Sometimes I think the worst are where no one but the victim can see. In some ways you've been lucky, hidden out here away from the rest of us. You've escaped being contaminated by human pollution. You still see clearly, respond honestly, and walk to the beat of your own heart. I've forgotten how. I've become a shark in a whirlpool with other sharks. What I want, I take because that's the only way to survive I know, and it's eating me alive. That's why I came here and am trying to set down roots. I want what you have and I'll be damned if I'll bring my world into yours. So for my sake and yours, let me play by your rules. For once in my life, let me do something right without compromising out of greed or need.''

Tears stung Lorelei's eyes as she gazed at him. So much pain—more in some ways than she herself suffered. She could no more refuse his request than she could stop her next heartbeat. ''I'm starving,'' she whispered, gently tugging his hands from her face. She made herself smile, silently denying the need that still burned in her body. Pushing at his chest, she tried to make room to slip to the floor.

Alex spanned her waist and set her on her feet. ''Thank you,'' he murmured, dropping a kiss on her forehead.

She shook her head. ''Thank you for caring enough not to take advantage of me.'' She walked carefully to the stove. ''We both know you could have.''

Alex traced the straight line of her spine. Despite the limp, Lorelei was one of the most graceful women he had seen. Everything about her was beautifully formed and molded. To take from her seemed almost a crime against nature. He smiled grimly at his thoughts. He hadn't realized moving to the country would suddenly turn him into a poet and resurrect old-fashioned traits that had little value in the marketplace. He went back to his salad bowl, remembering the arm twisting he had done while in Atlanta. The contract had been a mess of legal jargon that had covered stipulations angled for the other side of the table. He had fought hard and dirty to alter the deal they had been trying to jam down his throat. But this time his win had not brought a sense of accomplishment or triumph. All he had felt was weariness and relief that the fight was over. Brian had advised a change of life-style but he had said nothing about what happened when a man made such a switch. His health might benefit, but what was going to happen to the killer instinct that helped keep him at the top of the heap?

Lorelei lay in bed, thinking about the dinner she and Alex had shared. They had talked about her life and her training as an Olympic-bound athlete. Surprisingly, for the first time, she had found it possible to recall those days without feeling as though part of her had been stripped away to leave her raw, vulnerable, and useless. She had remembered the fun times, the moments of glory, the crazy glinches that sometimes occurred to ruin a beautiful routine. Once started, she had been unable to stop the outpouring of memories. Alex had listened, probing her mind, teasing her, bringing laughter to the telling and sympathy and compassion without pity to the ending.

It had been late when they had finished dinner, too late to ride home alone, according to Alex. They had turned Mystic loose to find his way back while Alex had driven her to the house. He had stayed only long enough to keep her company while she had unsaddled Mystic and obtained her promise to help him find a horse of his own and teach him to ride. She smiled softly, remembering his muttered comment about stupid impulses and city boys moving to the country and losing their minds in the transition.

Rolling over, she pressed her face into the pillow, feeling warm and oddly less alone. Until Alex had come into her life, she hadn't known she was lonely. Pippa was a wonderful aunt and friend but she had not been enough to fill up the empty places left by family and teammates. Her computers and the games she had invented had given her a purpose and a way to make the days roll by, but they had not filled the empty places, either. But Alex had. He teased her, made her laugh, and touched her heart. He made her hurt for him and what he was going through. He challenged her mind and forced her to unlock her emotions. He held out the apple of desire and offered her a bite—but only a little one. He cared about her. He offered her no promises and expected nothing from her but her time and presence. For now that was more than enough.

"I don't want a horse that big. Look at the thing. If I fall off I'll break my neck." Alex glared through the windshield at what looked like a small house on four legs. He wanted to spend time with Lorelei and was more than prepared to learn to ride to do it. What he wasn't ready to do was to spend time in a hospital with a broken something.

"Most people land on their rears."

"I don't care what part of my anatomy hits first—it's going to hurt from that height." He glanced at her, determined to win this battle.

Lorelei tried and failed to stifle her laughter. They were sitting in the car under the trees of the livestock auction yard. Without making a fuss, Alex had positioned them so that Lorelei could view the animals going on the block without having to fight the small crowd of people gathered for the same purpose.

"What about that little white one?" Alex demanded, his interest in her answer losing importance as he shared Lorelei's pleasure in the outing. He had wanted her to enjoy herself, to discover that she could take the next step out of the narrow boundaries of her life.

Lorelei knew without looking which one he meant. "She's too old."

"And less likely to feel like showing me who is boss," he returned promptly.

"You don't want a broken-down horse."

"I want a cushioned saddle on a rocking horse," he corrected, slanting her a grin that mocked his ignorance.

"You want the black gelding." Lorelei had contacted the local vet earlier in the week and had him stop at the auction barn to check over the mounts available. He had been very clear on which horses were the best offerings. A couple of Pippa's friends had provided information on previous owners and traits, giving Lorelei a fairly accurate picture of each animal. She had chosen accordingly and was determined to convince Alex to agree.

Alex sighed, casting one more look over the half-filled corral. "That thing looks big as a house."

"He has smooth gaits and he's just under eight years old. He'll be a good mount. He's used to beginners because he belonged to a girl who joined one of our local riding clubs. He was her first horse."

Alex glanced at her carefully, timing his next words. Oddly, now that it was time to put his plan into action, he discovered he was nervous. Suppose he was wrong. Suppose something went wrong. "I'll make a deal with you. I'll shut up about that monster if you'll keep me company while I do my bidding."

Lorelei turned her head sharply, shocked at the suggestion. "I can't," she responded automatically, casting a swift, wistful glance at the corral and the milling occupants.

Alex caught the look and almost grinned with relief. He had a chance. "Why not? There isn't much of a crowd and you don't have to walk far to get to the bleachers. The ground is smooth and you said yourself that the gelding would be one of the first horses up, and the horses were the first group of animals on the program. You won't be out there long enough to get tired."

Lorelei stared at him, hoping he was teasing

and knowing he was not. His eyes had never been more serious. She glanced back at the people beginning to fill the wooden plank seats around the small arena. She felt as if she were caught in a severe storm of stage fright. Her first competition hadn't been so difficult. But more importantly, she discovered something deeper than the tension, something surprising. She *wanted* to walk in the sun with Alex, sit in the bleachers, and bid for his horse. She looked at him, finding him watching her, waiting, silently promising her support all the way whatever her decision.

"I'll be right beside you all the way," he promised quietly, feeling her tension and the conflict going on within her. He slipped his hand over her clenched fists, threading his fingers through hers as they slowly relaxed.

Lorelei looked down at their hands and knew she was going to get out of the car and walk into that crowd. The decision had been long in coming and she would not let a little fear keep her from doing what had to be done if she were ever to be free. She had been a prisoner of her own and others' erroneous beliefs in her physical capabilities long enough. The scars that had made others point and stare were gone. She had one little limp and a funny voice. So what?

"All right," she agreed, breathing deeply while forcing her body to relax.

He squeezed her hand, but didn't let it go. "They say the first time is always the hardest."

"I'll remind you of that when you hit the ground the first time," she replied, attempting to tease.

His grin and the admiration in his eyes rewarded her for the effort. "Come on, woman. Let's go get me a horse." He leaned across the seat to kiss her, catching her unawares. Meaning only to touch her, he found her mouth too enticing for the simple, almost affectionate, caress he had intended. His arm slid around her waist drawing her close as her lips opened beneath his.

Lorelei responded to his kiss, forgetting the crowd, the auction, and what they had come to do. When he touched her, she felt beautiful, whole and free. His hand spoke of desire, his lips of passion. She wanted more than a taste of both. Moaning softly, she sought to deepen the contact. His groan of need was heady, a goad to her own desire. She twisted in his arms, stealing the space between them until her breasts flattened against his chest, the nipples pressing into the warmth as though they had come home.

Alex snatched at his dwindling control, reminding himself where they were and how close they were skirting the edge of restraint. He pulled back, hating the need. Lorelei's eyes were closed, her face glowing with the passion that had burned between them. "Woman, you go to my head quicker than the finest liquor," he muttered ruefully.

Lorelei lifted her lashes to stare into his eyes. "Should I be sorry?" she asked huskily.

"No!"

She smiled softly at the swift response. "Then that's all right."

Alex stroked her back, his fingers tracing the sleek contours as he calmed himself. "We seem to pick the strangest places to start fires we can't use."

"Bad timing."

"Bad planning." He leaned his head against hers for a moment, knowing that he could no longer touch her without making sure she understood how it was with them. "I want you so badly I ache. And you seem to want me." He raised his head to watch her carefully. "Are you sure this is what you want?"

Lorelei didn't hesitate. "I'm sure. Why won't you believe me?"

"Maybe I'm afraid to."

"Do you think that I'll demand something of you?" Lorelei wasn't sure what made her ask the question, but his change of expression made her realize that somehow she had guessed right.

"Maybe."

"And if I promise you I won't?"

He touched her face, tracing the fine bones of her jaw. His emotions were in a turmoil. He wasn't sure what he wanted anymore. He hated the out-of-control feeling, but he couldn't seem to get a handle on it no matter how much he tried. "Maybe I want you to need me. Maybe I'm afraid that you will. Maybe I don't want to wake up one day and figure out that I was simply an attractive man available to you when you decided to rejoin the land of the living.'' With another woman he would never have put his doubts into words.

Lorelei stared at him, stunned at vulnerability that she had never seen before. She was accustomed to knowing she had doubts and fears, but she hadn't thought in terms of anyone else, another sign of her stunted emotional growth. Moved by his words and her own need to wipe the uncertainty from his mind, she laid her fingers across his lips. ''I can't promise the future or even the present. I've learned that no promise is an armor against life and the tricks it pulls on us. But I can tell you that while I have not mixed with people much in recent years, I did earlier. You'd be surprised at the relationships that take place in competitive sports. The killing edge awakens emotions that don't seem to have a counterpart in ordinary life. That's why I stayed out of the running, even though I did have offers. I couldn't be . . .'' She hesitated, searching for the right word. ''. . . intimate with a man if I could not like the person, trust him, respect him.'' She shook her head, not happy with her explanation but lacking the experience to make it clearer. ''It's not a case of lust, damn it,'' she finished in a rush.

Alex looked into her eyes, seeing that untainted clarity that he admired and wished he still had. One by one, his doubts slipped away. His body relaxed as he kissed the fingertips of this woman who had given him a measure of peace. "Thank you."

She shook her head, her eyes misting. "No. You have given me too much for that to be a word between us. I'm not brave, but you make me feel that way." She glanced at the crowd. "I don't really want to get out of this car, but I'm going to, with you. You make it possible for me to try again."

She turned her head until their eyes met. Neither spoke for a long moment, both knowing that nothing would ever be quite the same again. Regardless of the future, whether they made love or not, both would remember this day and what they had given to each other.

# EIGHT

"Relax." Alex tucked Lorelei's arm more securely in the crook of his elbow, smiling as she glanced at him.

"I had a lot less trouble on a balance beam with the worst judges staring at my every move," she muttered, trying not to notice the interested looks they were receiving. "I feel like one of those animals on the block."

"You look sexy in the denims, and that long braid down your back is probably making every man here wonder what it would be like to have a wife or girlfriend with hair as long as yours."

She grinned at the mildly lecherous tone. "I don't think that's quite what any of them are thinking."

"But it made you smile." He stopped in front of the bleachers. "Now, where shall we sit?"

Lorelei glanced at the ten-tiered stand. "The third row will be fine."

Alex eyed the crowd, picking a spot with the least amount of people to step over or around. Going first, he did his best to shield Lorelei without making his efforts obvious. As he lurched over one of the boards between the seats, he tried not to show his concern that the planks were less than even and not especially secure.

Lorelei settled into the place she had chosen with a pleased sigh. "I did it," she mumbled, more to herself than to Alex.

Alex wrapped his arm around her shoulders as he took his place beside her. "I'd buy two horses and ride them both for that. I had no idea these seats would turn out to be lethal weapons or that I would be the one stumbling."

Lorelei laughed, and squeezed his arm. Delight in the step she had taken and the man responsible for it filled her, bringing a surge of joy so intense she wanted to laugh aloud. "If there was a gym near here I'd coach you on the beam. This is a piece of cake compared to that." She stopped when she realized what she had said.

"Better?" Alex asked, watching her intently.

"More than I would have believed possible. It didn't hurt."

The slamming of the heavy hammer against a

large bell shattered the mood, making Alex swear as Lorelei started. The auction had begun.

Lorelei stared at the gelding in the stall next to Mystic. When she had offered to teach Alex to ride she had forgotten one important item. There was no barn on his property; hence his horse, now dubbed Bouncer, was in her stable. Lorelei leaned on the top rail of the stall smiling at the memory of Alex's insistence that his animal have a name befitting his role in Alex's life.

"I'm probably going to be bouncing in and out, with the emphasis on the 'out' part, of the saddle more than I want to remember. So he deserves a handle that gives him half the credit for my soon-to-be-sore anatomy," he had muttered while trying to get the gelding out of the horse trailer they had taken to the auction.

"That smile is definitely new," Pippa murmured, coming to join Lorelei in looking over the new arrival. "He's a nice-looking beast. Alex did well at the auction. I hope he didn't have to pay over what he was worth."

"We didn't."

Pippa shot Lorelei a sharp look. "We?"

Lorelei kept her eyes on the horse. "I went with him."

"Hot dog!" Pippa shouted, throwing her arms around Lorelei's shoulders for a fierce hug. "I knew he would be good for you! I knew it!"

Lorelei hugged her back, feeling only marginally less enthusiastic. "I was so scared. It was like my first competition all over again."

"But you did it anyway. I'm proud of you, honey. After those damn reporters hounded you with all those prying questions and all those stupid friends of yours moaning and groaning about a few scars, I thought I would never see you go out again. Hell, I would have hidden in my room for the rest of my life after that mess. I was never so furious with my sister as I was the day I walked into that hospital room and heard her tell you that you shouldn't feel too bad just because you couldn't compete anymore. After all, coaches didn't have to be whole." Pippa snorted, her disgust and horror still as alive now as then. "That woman is a fool even if she is my own flesh and blood."

Lorelei shook her head as Pippa released her. "She didn't mean to hurt me."

"None of them did. That was what made it so awful. That's when I knew I had to get you out of there. The pity alone was enough to finish off a healthy woman, and you were little more than a hurt child."

"Well, it worked." Lorelei turned to head for the door. "I came here, put down roots, and went back to school."

"And built a career . . . and now you have a man in your life." Pippa matched her step to Lorelei's. "Or at least I hope so," she added, probing delicately.

Lorelei smiled slightly. "So it seems." She glanced at Pippa. "It was what you wanted."

"No, it was what I hoped. I like Alex. He strikes me as a tough customer, but there is something innately gentle about him that isn't quite hidden in spite of his best efforts."

"What do you know about why he moved out here instead of staying in Atlanta?"

The two women gained the house, entering by the side door. "Not much. Just what the local gossips had to say. He wanted a change of scene, a little more free time." Pippa filled a cup with coffee from the pot that was always warm. "Is there more?"

Lorelei hesitated, debating whether to share Alex's story. Only the fact that she needed to talk made her even consider the possibility. "Yes. He's under so much stress that it was beginning to affect his health. His father died of a heart attack when he was still young. Alex has been warned that he is heading in the same direction."

"Not good. That couldn't have been easy to take for a man with his kind of will. It would leave him feeling out of control of his life, off balance."

"One thing about living with a writer, I never have to cross my t's and dot my i's."

"So what are you going to do?"

"Go forward. I've come too far to want to draw back even if I could, which I'm not sure I could if I tried."

Pippa studied her niece. "You're coming awake."

"It's about time, don't you think?" Lorelei returned wryly. "Alex said I remind him of a sleeping princess. He's afraid that he just happens to be the prince around when I need the kiss."

"Fool!" Pippa frowned irritably. "Some men have all their brains in their shoes. He didn't see those half-naked sexy males running around flexing their muscles with whom you used to associate. If you were going to come down with a case of hormones you would have been more susceptible then than now. After all, the teen years are the worst possible time for control."

Lorelei started laughing. Whether it was Pippa's expression or her word choice, she couldn't stop chuckling even when the tears ran down her face and her stomach began to protest. "I'll tell him you said that," she gasped, striving for control.

"Do that. Might give the man some food for thought," she muttered, picking up her cup after refilling it. "I am going back to my book. At least my characters have sense enough to see what's under their noses . . ." She frowned darkly, already losing herself in the plot.

Still smiling, Lorelei went to the sink to wash her hands. It was her turn to start supper. As she worked she thought of Alex—his smile, his pleasure in her achievement today at the auction, and his sense of humor over his lack of riding ability. She knew, without him telling her, that the reason he had chosen to learn was that the sport gave her pleasure and that while she was on horseback she had the illusion of flawlessness. The fact that he would go to so much trouble for her warmed her, secretly delighted her, and yet at the same time frightened her. No one but Pippa and Jason had ever really seen her so clearly. She wasn't sure she was comfortable with Alex reading her so well. What would happen if she ultimately had something she wanted to hide from him?

"You really shouldn't," Lorelei protested, her hand on Bouncer's neck. The three of them stood in the middle of paddock, Alex astride the gelding and she on the ground. "Thirty minutes is enough for your first lesson. You have no idea how sore you'll feel by tonight."

Alex grinned, enjoying himself and not about to deny himself one minute with Lorelei. "I thought it would be harder than this. Except for getting the bit in his mouth and the cinch tight enough, I am doing better than I hoped. Besides, the sooner I master walking the sooner I can go on to other things, and ultimately you and I will be able to ride down by the lake. It can't be much fun for you to stand around watching me flop up and down in the saddle."

"You don't flop. You slide." She laughed at his indignant expression. "Sort of."

"At least I'm staying on." He picked up the reins and thumped the horse in the ribs as he had been instructed to do. Bouncer looked over his shoulder, twitched his ears, and started to amble in the direction of the corral gate. "I'm on a roll. This time I even got this thing going with one kick, not four."

Lorelei turned, following his progress. She had to admit Alex was doing well with his lessons. He had a quick mind coupled with the intensity that she had first sensed in him. "Back straight, toes in, heels more level. You're going to lose a stirrup if you aren't careful."

Alex obeyed, concentrating on his posture and keeping the horse moving in the wide circle that Lorelei had decreed. Lorelei turned easily, her eyes on Alex. He looked good on Bouncer and oddly more relaxed than she had ever seen him. There was no doubting his determination to learn to ride, and learn quickly. They worked together for another half hour before Lorelei called a halt. Alex managed to guide the gelding to her to dismount. He grimaced on sliding to the ground.

"I feel like I've been sitting astride a house," he muttered, trying without success to straighten his legs.

Lorelei frowned at him, worry lining her brow. "I should never have let you stay on him that long."

Grimacing, Alex walked a few of the kinks out. "It wasn't your fault, so stop looking so unglued. I'll survive. Serves me right for going hell-bent for leather, as Brian would say. One of these days I'll learn to take things slow.''

''I'll take Bouncer in and get him unsaddled and brushed down.''

Alex walked awkwardly over to pull the reins out of Lorelei's hands. ''No, you won't. I distinctly remember your telling me that a rider tacks out his own horse and sees to his needs before his own. I rode that black cuss, I'll take care of the rest of it.''

''I hate stubborn men,'' Lorelei mumbled, following Alex's bow-legged progress to the barn.

''Know many?'' He glanced over his shoulder to grin at her.

''A few bullheaded coaches.''

''They don't count. This is a new game now.''

They entered the barn, the dimness closing in on them. The smell of horse and hay was pleasant, earthy. Lorelei stopped at the equipment closet to pick up curry brushes and wipe cloths. By the time she arrived at Bouncer's stall, Alex had the gelding unsaddled and was struggling with changing the bridle to a halter.

''Doing anything tonight?'' Alex asked as he dropped the head gear over the hook outside the stall.

''No, why?''

''I thought we might have dinner at my place. Alone. I'll cook.'' He turned, his eyes searching hers in the soft light.

Lorelei would have accepted his words at face

value but for that look. She read the banked desire and knew that Alex's restraint was finally gone. He was offering her much more than a meal this time. There would be no turning back if she agreed to come to him. "You might not be up to it by then." Lorelei looked at him, knowing she was going to accept even as she put up a token protest.

"That's an excuse."

"I'd like to," she admitted slowly.

He touched her cheek, lightly stroking the ivory curve. "But?"

"But, oddly enough, I'm a little nervous."

"Of me?"

"Of both of us." She smiled slightly. "I like being with you. I'm almost afraid to believe how much."

He sighed deeply, unmanned by her honesty. He moved closer until his chest brushed her breasts. Still watching her, he drew her into his arms. "I like being with you, too. You know that. I thought we had agreed that it was what we both wanted."

"Agreeing and actually planning to do something are two different things. The other times have sort of just happened."

"Cold feet." He leaned his head against her hair, realizing he should have anticipated her reaction. "Will it be any better tomorrow?"

"Probably not," she whispered, burrowing nearer as the scent of man and horse surrounded her in a warm cocoon. "I told you I wasn't particularly brave."

"And I told you that was a load of garbage. I'm the idiot here. Not you. I meant to go slow and not push. I can't seem to remember that even in my ordinary life. Let alone with you." He hugged her, then started to step away.

Lorelei held on, denying his attempt to put some distance between them. "I don't know about your professional life, but I'm too cautious here. You're right and I'm not."

"I don't want you to think that I'm inviting you to my house only to . . ." He hesitated, annoyed at the blunt way he had been about to speak. This virgin business was a minefield of strange bombs, one of which was that plain speaking wasn't always the best policy.

"Get me into bed," Lorelei finished for him, a little surprised at the awkward way he had stopped talking.

He nodded, his lips twisting ruefully. "I should have known," he murmured more to himself than to her.

"What?" Lorelei tipped her head, curious at the odd tone in his voice.

"You have a way of cutting through to the heart of things, and here I was trying to spare your blushes." She laughed, a husky sound that went straight to Alex's very active and frustrated libido. This time, when he took her in his arms, there was nothing but passion driving him.

Lorelei lifted her face to his, her lips parting for the kiss she had been waiting for since he had arrived this morning. Her fingers threaded through his hair as his tongue stroked her lips, tasting, teasing, and enticing. She moaned deeply, leaning into his warmth, her hips tipping to cradle him intimately.

Alex tightened his hold, his eyes blazing with passion barely held in check. He wanted her. His hands roved over her back, pressing, molding her closer. He shifted, spreading his legs, taking as much of her weight as she would allow. Turning slightly without breaking the kiss, he slipped his hand between them, his fingers flicking open the buttons of her blouse.

"I have to touch," he whispered, raising his head just enough to speak. The glazed look in her eyes pleased him more than the most sultry look any woman had ever sent his way.

Lorelei stared at him, wanting, needing until her body felt on fire. "I want you to," she breathed.

His hand slid up her abdomen to the lacy bra cupping her breasts. He felt her swift gasp of response and smiled. His fingers traced the outline of lace, drifting from one cup to the other, coming close with each touch to the nipples straining at the fabric. When his fingers finally captured one peak, Lorelei jerked wildly in his arms. He took her mouth then, catching the moan of delight in his own. Caressing one tight nub then the other, he pleasured her even as his own desire reached painful levels. He wanted her to want him with the same madness that drove all thought but her image from his mind. But more than that he wanted her to know that only pleasure would be found in his arms, never pain, fear, or embarrassment.

"You're beautiful," he whispered huskily as he slipped her breasts free. He bent her gently over his arm, supporting her completely as he nuzzled the creamy flesh, his lips tracing the lush curves.

Lorelei closed her eyes, too carried away to care what he did as long as he didn't stop. She had never known such sensation existed. His teeth were sharp, tiny darts of pain instantly soothed by the warm bath of his tongue over her nipples. His breath was cool on her moist skin, making her ache for the next touch of his mouth. Without realizing it her hips began a rotation as old as Eve, a woman's dance to entice her mate to the height of insanity. Her hands dug into his shoulders, marking him as her own. Her head thrown back, she reveled in the feel of her body and his.

Alex lifted his head, desperately searching for a place to lie with her. He stared at the rugged interior of the barn, suddenly remembering where they were and how close he was to taking her in the dubious comfort of the hay. He swore once, his body screaming for the release it knew would not be coming. "Lorelei," he said roughly, stunned at the passionate expression on her face.

Her skin glowed a soft pink, her breath tiny pants indicating full arousal.

*What have I done?* he asked himself furiously. She was a virgin, someone he cared about. She was not a woman to be taken lightly on the ground without comfort or care.

Lorelei opened her eyes reluctantly. The taut, almost angry look on Alex's face stunned her. "What's wrong?" she asked, her voice breaking on the last word. For the first time she didn't notice the slip.

"I am. We can't. Not here. It isn't right."

"You want to stop?" She couldn't believe it. He was rejecting her again. Every sense was crying out for the fulfillment that only he could provide, and he was rejecting her.

"I have to stop before I hurt you," he corrected harshly. He lifted her into his arms, bringing her hips in total contact with his very rigid and demanding body. "Your first time deserves a better setting than this. A soft bed for one, and all the time and privacy you want. We don't have any of that."

She wrapped her arms around his neck, her eyes fierce. "I don't care."

"But I do." He shook her gently. "I've done a few things in my life that I regret, but hurting you in any way that I can help will never be one of them."

"You're hurting now."

"I'll survive."

"So will I."

He kissed her hard, stopping her protests with the only way left. For one moment he allowed all his frustrations to pour from his mouth to hers. Lorelei met his fire with a matching flame, her fingers spearing into his hair as she pitted her will to his. What she lacked in experience she made up for in determination. And still she lost. She could feel him slipping away before he raised his head.

"Come to me tonight," he commanded. "For dinner. For later. For whatever you want for as long as you will."

Lorelei was breathing heavily, her bare breasts brushing the fabric of his shirt with each inhalation. The sensation was erotic, intoxicating, fueling her desire to mind-boggling heights. Drunk on passion, she demanded a promise of her own. "No drawing back."

"No."

"Your word."

He laughed harshly. "Honey, I couldn't pull away like this one more time if my life depended on it. The only one who will have that option tonight will be you. I'm done being noble."

Lorelei searched his face, wondering at the uncertainty she saw. "You think I will?"

"I hope you won't."

"And if I did?"

"I'd come after you."

"Why?"

Alex hesitated, not sure he had an answer but knowing she needed one. "You matter to me. I touch you and I feel things I have never felt before."

"Pity?"

"I thought we were past that." Anger bit into his voice, stinging them both.

"I'm not like most of the people you know."

"Better than many. More than most."

She shook her head. "Naive."

"Honest."

"Inexperienced."

"Clean. Pure. Untainted."

"Sounds like a soap."

He shook her, his expression darkening. "Don't joke. Not now. I don't want what I've had. I like who and what you are. I wish I still had my ideals, trust, honesty without compromise. I lost or gave mine away a long time ago. You make me feel young, new, fresh. Don't think you are less than people like me. We're the losers, not you."

Lorelei saw then what she needed to see to help her make a decision based on more than her response to him as a man. Alex *needed* her. For the first time in a long time she had something to bring to a relationship. Pride and a kind of strength filled her at the thought. She smiled, her lips curving deeply, her body softening against his.

"I'll come."

Alex didn't understand what marker in their relationship they had passed, but he knew it was there. For now it was enough that she would share the night with him.

# NINE

Lorelei stared at her closet, debating what to wear. Excitement flowed in her veins like heady wine. The need to see Alex, to taste the passion he offered her was growing with each passing minute. She should have been afraid of the intimacy, or at least cautious about making herself vulnerable to a man. Yet she could feel no restraint. On some very important level she trusted Alex to be good to her, to care how she felt.

Her fingers settled on the fine cotton peasant dress that Pippa had brought home from one of her cruises. She had tried it on only once, disliking it the moment she had realized the scooped neck revealed the pale silver line that was the only scar on her throat left from the accident. If it had been anyone else but Alex who was to see her, she would not have even considered the dress despite its attractive figure-clinging style and flattering deep-rose color. Smiling faintly at her need to let him see her as she was, she took the gown from the closet and slipped it over her head. For the first time, she blessed the fact that Pippa had insisted that she have an array of cosmetics despite her reclusive ways.

"Lori, are you dressed?" Pippa called through the closed door.

"Come on in," Lorelei replied, frowning. "I just realized I don't have a mirror in here. I'll need to get one."

"That's why I'm here. Use this."

Lorelei turned, catching sight of what Pippa was holding. "That looks like an antique, and a valuable one at that."

Pippa barely glanced at the ornate oval looking glass. "It's a gift. I'm been saving it for your debut."

Lorelei stared at her, touched by the gift and the love of the giver. "You have given me so much."

Pippa shook her head. "No. We have given to each other. I was well on my way to becoming a bit of a hermit until you came here. I had to start thinking of someone besides myself. That was good." She shrugged, vaguely uncomfortable. "Besides, I was lonely. Not that I'll ever admit that to anyone but you," she added fiercely.

Lorelei felt the sting of tears and blinked them back. "Your secret is safe with me."

"It had better be." She handed Lorelei the mirror. "Do you like it?"

"Who wouldn't? It's gorgeous." Lorelei peered at herself, finding it easier to study her face without focusing on the scar or the memory of those which no longer existed to mar her skin in some places and still remained in others.

"I'll leave you to get ready."

Lorelei caught Pippa's arm before she could go. "No, stay. I may have all the pots and jars to make myself beautiful for Alex, but I don't have the first idea about what to do with them. You always look exquisite. Help me."

Pippa laughed softly, a faint tinge of red blooming in her artfully made-up cheeks. "I love makeup. You know that."

Lorelei sat down, placing her new mirror firmly in the middle of her dressing table. "Well, do your stuff. I want to knock Alex's eyes out."

Pippa's brows rose at the declaration. "I think you've already managed that without any help from me." She reached for the moisturizer. "From what I've seen, you have that guy hooked and he seems happy to be caught, which is even more important." She spread on a thin film, watching Lorelei as she worked. "I can tell you're happy as well. I'm glad."

"You don't think I'm rushing things?"

"I never have felt counting minutes in a relationship was much of an advantage. I've met people I've only known for a few days and realized I could trust them with my life. And others with whom I have been acquainted for years that I wouldn't let babysit my cat if I had one. Emotions can be our greatest asset if we allow ourselves to listen to our hearts. Alex is a good man. He's tough but he's fair, and anyone with eyes can see that he cares for you. I'd say go for whatever feels good to you both."

Their eyes met, the younger searching the older's. "My mother wouldn't agree with you."

"My sister thinks with her pecs, or whatever muscles she's developing this week."

"He's not thinking of marriage."

"Is any man? Are you?" Pippa began blending in eye shadow on Lorelei's lids. "You are just now climbing out of your shell. Don't be in such a rush to curl up in another one."

"You sound like you're for an affair."

"It isn't for me to decide. I will say this: It wouldn't hurt you, or him come to that. Alex, for my money, is entirely too caught up in his business. He could use a little enjoyment in his life. And what's the harm? You're both free."

Lorelei grinned, suddenly feeling the last tiny doubt slip away. "You know, I was sort of worried you would think I was acting the fool." She chuckled at Pippa's shocked expression.

"Me? Honey, I wrote the book on foolishness. I'm the one who moved out of the parents' house at eighteen and tramped around Europe on my own for a year. Then worked in Alaska as a short-order cook and on a cruise ship as a cabin girl before I settled here and built this place. I love my independence and I have given anyone who tried to take it away from me trouble. I don't do anything I think anyone else wants me to do. I hate following orders and I detest deadlines. I write stuff that most people wouldn't even consider literature. Don't expect me to try to play the heavy parent. It isn't in my makeup. You're a very intelligent woman. Experienced or not, you can make your own decisions, so you should. The devil with what the rest of the world thinks.'' Pippa stepped back. ''Take a look at that face and tell me this woman doesn't know what she wants and how to get it.''

Lorelei stared at her reflection, seeing a woman with more beauty than she had known she possessed. Pale eyes gazed back at her, bold, oddly unafraid of the world.

''Remember, you have more strength than most. You've challenged the Fates and won. You want something—go for it. Whether you win or lose you will never be down for the count. You will survive.'' Pippa bent, giving Lorelei a swift hug before leaving without another word.

Lorelei hardly noticed her departure, although Pippa's words lingered to bolster the confidence that Alex had planted within her. He was waiting. The man she had chosen, the one who had chosen her. It was time. She rose, her hand steady as she collected her wrap and purse. This time she would take the car, not Mystic. This time she would walk in the front door, not hide in the shadows. This time she would step into his arms without waiting for him to make the first move.

"I didn't think you were com—" Alex froze, his sentence half finished as he stared at Lorelei as she stood poised on the threshold. "Woman, you're beautiful," he whispered in awe as he reached for her.

Lorelei dropped her purse, the fleecy shawl across her shoulders slipping to the porch as she simply walked into Alex's arms. "I hope so. I wanted to be," she breathed, feeling his warmth enfold her. She raised her head, her lips parting to receive his kiss. Her eyes were soft, inviting, bewitching.

Alex was lost even had he wanted to be strong. "Don't look at me like that."

"Like how?"

"Like you would die for my mouth."

She traced his lips, smiling faintly. "But I would," she said huskily. "It gives me such pleasure. Your taste is more intoxicating than wine."

Alex groaned as he bent his head, at the same time kicking the door shut to the outside world. "I wanted to woo you a little," he protested even as he took her mouth, satisfying them both. At first his kiss was gentle, a tentative caress, but that wasn't enough for either of them.

Lorelei felt his arms tighten as she pressed closer, her arms sliding around his waist. A heavy ache spread throughout her body, intensifying as Alex deepened the kiss. She yielded to the ache, knowing that the closer she came to Alex's strength, the greater the pleasure. Her mouth opened to the fierce demand of his, and all her senses filled with him.

What she felt was more than all that had gone before. There was no past to mar the beauty of the moment, no present to intrude, and no future to steal the joy of their passion. There was only now, this man in this quiet place.

His hands slid down her back to her hips, shaping the rounded flesh and pulling her nearer until she could feel the swelling demand of his body. Her hands clutched at his back, unconsciously commanding his possession. She gasped as he swung her into his arms and strode down the hall. Her head fell back over his arms, her eyes locked with his. The taut, primitive stamp of a man's claim of his woman was on his features. She gloried in the look and the power of knowing that she had put that feeling on his face. Just for one instant, as Alex laid her down on his bed, she knew a flash of panic at the unknown stretched before her. Then she looked into his eyes and saw the gentleness and understanding that seemed always to be there when she needed it the most.

"Your choice, Lorelei," he whispered, making no move to seduce or hold her against her will.

She lifted her arms without hesitation. "I choose you. I came tonight for this and you. I will not, I do not, regret my decision."

Alex closed his eyes against the relief making him light-headed. For one moment he had been afraid she would demand her freedom. "I'm glad." The simple words didn't cover the myriad of emotion pulling at him, but it was the best he could do as he stared at her kiss-swollen lips and soft body. He eased down on the bed beside her, carefully staying on the side opposite her weak one. "I like this dress, but I have a yen to see you without it," he said, stroking the gathered neckline off her shoulders. It slipped down her arms, inch by inch, to reveal the lush fullness of her breasts barely cupped in champagne lace. Her nipples were tiny rosebuds waiting for him to pluck.

Lorelei shifted as he teased the peaks, a moan whispering in the half gloom. "The light. Turn it off," she said, twisting nearer.

"I want to see you."

She caught his wrists. "Not tonight. Please."

He turned his hands until he could thread his fingers between hers. "It barely shows, and then only when the light hits it a certain way." He glanced briefly at the pale scar on her throat, then dismissed it.

She shook her head, hating the tension invading her body. "My leg . . ." she began awkwardly. "It's not pretty."

His eyes softened on seeing her distress. He settled beside her, cuddling rather than holding her. "I could quote all sorts of fancy promises, but I won't. You will have to trust me when I tell you I don't care about the scars. I do care that you were hurt, in pain, and that fools in your past hurt you by turning from you because of those wounds. But I don't care if you aren't physically perfect. Those marks don't change the woman you are. They don't make me want you less or ache for your touch any less fiercely. I want to make love to you, not your leg, not your scars, but to the woman who rode out of the mist and looked at me with the most wary eyes I have ever seen, the woman I thought could not speak, the woman who shows me more pleasure in a simple kiss than the most accomplished bedmate I have ever had. That isn't a pretty speech or one I have ever used. It is simply the truth."

Fear blossomed at his demand she trust him enough not to come to him in darkness. She knew he would make love to her in the shadows if she forced it, but she knew, too, that something would be lost between them, something valuable, something, perhaps, irreparable. Slowly, her hold loosened. As she gave him his freedom she earned her own in inches as he lowered his hands and eased up the fabric of her skirt. The scars on her upper leg were extensive from the damage of the accident and the repair work which hadn't always gone well. Two discolored lines ran on either side of her limb, the kneecap was a cross-stitched quilt of surgical skill.

Alex felt searing rage at the pain she must have endured as he stared at the puckered marks. He reached out, his fingers lightly tracing the long lines until his palm cupped her knee. Only then did he raise his eyes to hers. The vulnerability, the wariness in her gaze made him ache to wipe the damage of the past from her mind.

"I didn't faint, and I still want you," he said, his hand stroking her tense leg as he spoke. "With the lights or without, you're still beautiful."

Lorelei searched his eyes, seeing the truth. Tears filled hers—relief, freedom, grief that she could not be whole for him. He brushed her cheeks, sipping at the moisture, taking it into his mouth as his fingers moved over her scars, touching each one as though it were a precious part of her. He gathered her into his arms, kissing the tears from her eyes as he held her close. "One of these days we'll go swimming together. You'll wear a tiny bikini that will make me wish we were here in this room and we'll play in the water like otters."

She almost believed him. "How did you know I hadn't been?"

He smiled sadly. "You haven't been anywhere, my lover. But you will go now, with me." He lifted her up higher in the bed, his hands cupping her breasts as he eased his weight over her body.

Suddenly Lorelei realized what he meant to do.

She stiffened as she felt his mouth on the first of her scars. "No, please."

He lifted his head. "I will please you. I'm going to kiss every inch of you and start a fire I hope will burn us both to cinders. I'm starting here." His fingers dipped into the lacy cups, teasing her nipples so that she gasped in pleasure, forgetting the flaws as she felt the flames begin. "Before the night is over, I'll be so deep inside you and you so close to my heart that neither of us will ever be the same again."

Lorelei caught his shoulders as his lips traced patterns of delight on first one leg then the other. His breath was hot, his teeth gentle, his hands deliciously tormenting. Lorelei couldn't breathe, but she didn't care. All she knew was the fire and the sudden coolness of her naked flesh a moment before Alex pulled himself up her body to take her lips. The dress slipped over her head almost before she realized it as she fumbled for the buttons on his shirt.

Alex caught her hands, stilling her tentative caresses. "Wait, love. Let me love you first, just this one time." He looked deep into her eyes, willing her to trust him in this as she had with her scars.

Lorelei curled her fingers into fists against his skin, barely understanding what he was asking of her or why. She could not deny that look in his eyes, that plea which was half command.

"Just this once, I promise, my siren of the mist." He bent his head to tease her lips.

Lorelei sighed at his touch, relaxing. Her fingers unclenched as she softened against him. A strange, almost terrifying wave of emotion swept over her. Her eyes widened as his hands drifted over her thighs, caressing, guiding. Tension built, driving out the need to examine the intense feelings building within her. All she could do was lie in his arms, following where he led into the uncharted vastness of her unexplored passions. She cried out as a surge of sheer pleasure caught her unawares. Alex lifted his head, his eyes gleaming at the sounds coming from her lips. His mouth ghosted lower, nipping, tasting, moving ever nearer to the heart of her desire. Her scent bewitched him, building his own passion to fever pitch. Wanting became pain even as he denied himself to make her first time the most beautiful it was in his power to give her.

Lorelei searched wildly for Alex's face as the tension tightened and fear laced the passion at the change in the body she thought she knew so well. "Alex," she gasped, focusing on him as he seared her breasts with his lips and stroked the throbbing flesh between her legs with a touch that was gentle yet demanding. She arched, twisting for the union she had never known.

In some far corner of her mind, Lorelei knew she was close to losing herself in his passion. Nothing could exist in this vibrantly alive world without burning up from the intensity of feeling. She whispered his name again and again as waves of delight poured over her burning flesh, bringing an even greater tension until a sudden burst of sheer pleasure snapped the ties binding her to earth and threw her into a place she had never known before. Her body quivered helplessly in the aftershock, her mind stunned at the experience.

His name slipped past her lips, her need to be sheltered by him in the quivering breath. Alex got up, hastily pulling his clothes off before coming back to take Lorelei in his arms again.

He rose over her, joining their flesh in a glide so smooth she felt nothing more than the silken heat of his maleness completing her existence. In the soft light he was dark, strong, and yet so gentle with her that tears slipped from her eyes at the beauty.

"Remember this," Alex commanded huskily. "Remember this moment and know that I wanted you more than life itself. You are beautiful, my lady of silence. Remember that and us together in this moment."

Lorelei gasped as he flexed, his flesh seeming to grow within her, stretching her until the sweet tension built again, only higher and brighter than before. Her hands slipped up his shoulders, pulling him down into the cradle of her softness. Impatience drove her as she twisted beneath him, seeking the glorious fire that had burned her so indelibly.

Alex groaned and began moving. The fierce control over his body was lost in her feminine demand. She was a moist satin sheath, holding him snugly as her slender legs wrapped around his hips so demandingly that she drove him beyond the edge of restraint. The physical pleasure of possession flashed to a driving need to become one with her, to be so deeply buried in her flesh as to penetrate to the very heart of all that she was. He needed her.

Lorelei responded to each thrust with more abandon than she would have believed herself capable of had she been thinking clearly. Every undulation of her hips was a passionate demand for more of him. The Lorelei of the past and the shadows came alive until nothing of the recluse remained. This was the Lorelei that could have been—wild, uninhibited, and free.

Lorelei was unaware of her wild cries or the birth of her power. All she knew was the perfection she had found in Alex's arms. For this moment in time, she had stopped the march of the clock. For this instant, Alex was hers and she gloried in knowing that she alone could give him the intensity of feeling that brought the groans of pleasure and need to his lips. His harsh gasp answered her own calls for the ultimate completion. She arched higher, meeting his most powerful thrust with the last ounce of her strength. The sun seemed to nova between them, the flames engulfing and consuming all energy, all sound, all movement. She fell back against the bed, helpless in Alex's arms as she was granted her release. He slumped over her, protecting her with his body as his own went limp with satisfaction and fulfillment.

Alex caught his breath, his eyes closed, his head pillowed against Lorelei's breasts. Nothing that had gone before had prepared him for what had occurred between them. His hands lightly traced the soft mounds near his lips, feeling the shivers of passion that raced over Lorelei's skin. Slowly, he raised his head, hoping that she was as moved by the experience as he. He had not meant to lose control in the end, becoming more rough with the force of the need she had built within him than he had bargained for.

"Are you all right?" he questioned softly, searching her face. The silver tracks left by her tears were visible in the muted light. He touched them lightly. "Did I hurt you?"

"No." She read the anxiety in his eyes. "You made me feel more beautiful than I have ever felt in my life. Thank you."

He cupped her face in his palms, his thumbs pressing her lips closed. "Not 'thank you.' It was mutual. You gave me more pleasure than I have ever known." He smiled at the open skepticism in her eyes. "You don't have enough experience to know what we shared was rare. You were like living fire in my arms."

Her smile was shy, tentative. He watched it

bloom on her lips and knew that he had never seen a sight so moving. For the first time he saw in her a woman beginning to feel confidence in her femininity. His pride, his ego, call it what you will, grew with Lorelei's smile. To know that he had given her more than pleasure pleased him more than he could have said or even expected. Rolling on his side, he cradled her, knowing he could not tell her how much she meant to him, knowing that perhaps even he did not know how much as yet.

# TEN

Lorelei lay in Alex's arms, knowing she had to get up and dress. It was time to go home. But she couldn't make herself move. Shifting closer to his warmth, she tried to analyze her feelings, to rationalize her need to stay near to him.

Alex turned on his side. "Talk to me. I know you're not sleeping."

"I should go."

"Why?"

"My aunt . . ."

"Knows you're with me," he finished for her. "Do you need space? Is that it? I tried not to rush you."

Lorelei heard the self-directed anger in his voice and reacted before she thought. "No, it isn't that.

It's just . . ." She hesitated, feeling foolish. "I don't know what to do next."

Alex searched her face, unable to believe it could be so simple a problem. He had lain beside her, fully aware that she could be regretting their lovemaking. He had been surprised at his own reactions to the thought. He hadn't wanted Lorelei to ever regret anything they did. He had wanted her to know how important she was to him, but he hadn't known how to tell her. Her answer had been a relief in more ways than one. For now she needed lightness, not the burden of emotions that he didn't understand himself.

"Next, you lie in my arms and tell me what a great lover I am," he murmured, watching her closely. Her quick look, her surprise coupled with the relaxation of her body, told him he had chosen just the right tactic. "And I'll tell you how gorgeous you are and we'll see what else pops up in the conversation."

Lorelei laughed, the earthy humor appealing to her. "That's terrible."

Alex rolled onto her, trapping her even though she had not tried to escape. His body responded instantly, shocking him anew with the desire she aroused with just a look and a soft laugh. "You didn't think so earlier."

"A slight aberration on my part," she teased, smiling.

"Only slight?" Dark brows arched over wickedly twinkling eyes.

She giggled, feeling younger with every word. Impulsively, her fingers danced over his skin, seeking and finding a ticklish spot or two. Alex jerked in reflex.

"Woman, you are looking for trouble."

"Is that what I was doing?" Lorelei returned innocently, the gleam in her eyes telling a different story.

Alex captured her lips, delving into their sweetness before Lorelei could evade him. When they were both breathless he lifted his head, a mischievously male grin tilting his lips. "I think I created a wanton."

Lorelei arched against him, teasing him with her body. She couldn't believe her own boldness. "You don't like?" she whispered throatily.

"You know damn well I do," he groaned, this time the smoldering fire in his eyes having nothing to do with humor. His hands moved over her body with sure intent.

Lorelei gave herself up to the magic he created, learning, in the hours that followed, the depth of his tenderness as he pleasured her without irritating her tender, newly awakened body. Learning, too, of the ways to touch him, to bring the most pleasure and ultimately fulfillment for them both.

Lorelei stood at her bedroom window, looking toward the trees which hid Alex's house from view. He was in Atlanta for the next two days. She had spent the night before with him as she had every night this week. She missed him already despite the knowledge that he would be back soon. Her work had not kept her occupied today and she couldn't seek forgetfulness in her bed, for sleep was eluding her. Even a ride in the moonlight held no appeal. She paced her room, needing an outlet for the energy and restlessness plaguing her. Every third round she would stop beside the phone hoping he would call and knowing he wouldn't. The labor-dispute situation that had taken him to the city was complicated, requiring many meetings, possibly through the night, to resolve. Sighing, she sat down on the bed just as the phone rang. She grabbed it, her eyes alight with pleasure. Her glow died at the sound of her mother's voice on the line.

"Lori, how are you, dear? Your father and I have been worried. We haven't heard from you in a while. Are you all right?"

"Of course I am, Mother. Pippa or I would have called you if something had happened." Lorelei frowned at the overly concerned tone of her mother, feeling vaguely guilty for not remembering to place her weekly call to her relatives to report on her physical status. Even after all these years they seemed incapable of believing that, apart from a few marks on her skin, her health was good. Her lips tilted in a faint smile at the realization that she had chosen Alex's words to describe her scars.

"My sister always has her head in those stories

she writes. I doubt that she'd know if anything happened to you unless she fell over the body,'' the older woman responded tartly, then sighed. ''I'm sorry. That wasn't nice, and I do appreciate what Pippa has done for you. Really I do.''

Startled at her apology, Lorelei's frown returned. ''Mother, are you all right?''

''Of course I am. It's just that this wedding has all of us on edge. I don't excel at this kind of thing and your brother and that girl want a big, splashy do.''

''What wedding, Mother? This is the first I've heard of anyone getting married.''

''I'm sure I wrote you.''

''If you did, I didn't get the letter,'' Lorelei stated flatly.

''Damn the post office. I bet they'll mess up delivering the invitations as well. Gene will be furious, and I don't even want to think what his fiancée will say. The girl makes me feel positively inadequate. Everyone in the family knows I'm at my best in the physical arena. I can't be the society matron that young woman expects. I can't help not being on a par with her family.''

Lorelei wasn't sure whether to laugh or cry through the disjointed speech. Clearly the youngest of her clan was contemplating a trip down the aisle with a woman of a heritage-conscious family who, if her mother's hints were to be believed, was a snob. Trying to picture lanky, good-natured, slightly-uncoordinated-except-when-he-was-running-track Eugene bound for life to such a paragon boggled the mind.

"When he is tying the knot?" she asked.

"Three months from now. Which is one of the reasons why I am calling. His family wants to meet all of us, and that includes you and Pippa. Knowing how both of you feel about leaving your little hideaway in the woods, I think it would be best all around if we came to you. Say this weekend."

"You can't be serious," Lorelei exclaimed, visions of previous thoroughly uncomfortable, though, fortunately widely spaced, visits filling her memory.

"Now, Lori, don't be difficult. There will only be six of us, and that house of Pippa's will easily expand that far for two days."

"I don't see why—" She got no further as her mother interrupted, the verbal bit firmly between her teeth.

"Put Pippa on."

Lorelei tried one more time. "Mother, you can't seriously expect to drop in on Pippa this way."

"It won't be for long and it's for your brother," her mother countered determinedly.

Lorelei sighed, knowing she was defeated unless Pippa could come up with an excuse to forestall the descent of her well-meaning but definitely irritating relatives. "Hold on while I get Pippa," she murmured.

\* \* \*

"Your mother wants to do what?" Pippa demanded irritably. She glanced at her computer and the half page that had been giving her such trouble showing on the screen. "I've just gotten a handle on my plot problem. I don't have time for Gail's crazy schemes right now. What the devil do we have to do with Eugene unless this girl and her family are checking for hereditary defects, and if she is, she won't find them here." She punched out her program and stalked to the door. "I know what is prompting this. One good case of I can't cope with parenting and housekeeping. Gail always was good at getting someone else to bail her out of her problems. Well, this time it won't be me. I will not have my weekend messed up for this kind of nonsense!" She entered Lorelei's room and snatched up the phone.

"I will not have it," she said decisively without giving Gail a chance to get in her tale of woe. "I mean it, Gail. You tell this girl and her family that this little junket is not on. I am right in the middle of a book and I am not going to put up with visitors. The woman is marrying Eugene, not us."

Lorelei leaned against the door, trying not to laugh. Watching her mother and Pippa lock horns had never been amusing until tonight. Pippa, by her own admission, was amazingly self-centered where her work was concerned. Her mother was equally selfish about her family and getting her own way. Neither was good at backing down.

"No, we won't come there. At least *I* won't," she amended, glancing at Lorelei.

Lorelei shook her head, no more eager to give up her weekend than Pippa. Alex and she had gone to a video arcade, the animal auction, and to a restaurant that had just opened up in the next town. She had enjoyed the trips once she had gotten over a bout or two of nerves, but she was in no mood to face her family, gathered for the express purpose of being inspected for suitability.

"I know all about family feeling, Gail." Pippa grimaced at the words pouring in her ear. "Of course we care."

Lorelei stepped closer feeling the battle shift in her mother's favor.

"I realize how important this is to Eugene." Pippa looked at Lorelei.

Lorelei spread her hands, beginning to feel as guilty as Pippa seemed.

"You promise you'll leave on Sunday night?" Pippa asked, her expression resigned. She listened for a moment before nodding. "All right. Come early Saturday. I'll put you all up for one night and that's it. And, Gail, I mean it. You try to stay a second longer than you promised and I'll make such a scene that this girl and her family will never speak to any of us again. I am on deadline. I can't give you any more time than this, and Lorelei is in the same fix with her latest game." She hung up a moment later, a muttered curse emphasizing the bang of the phone into its cradle.

"You tried," Lorelei consoled her aunt while wondering how she was going to explain to Alex that he had to stay away until her family left. She had a sinking feeling he wouldn't like the idea at all.

"And look how far it got me."

"It could be worse. Mother might have had in mind a week and a gathering of the whole clan."

Pippa rolled her eyes. "Even Gail wouldn't have the nerve for that after the last visit. Of all the asinine stunts, that was the topper. Trying to get you to aim for the show circuit with Mystic, with an eye for the Olympia equestrian team. I swear, if I wasn't sure Mom loved Dad I would think Gail adopted. The woman has the brains and sensitivity of an ant. Did she think you were going to give up your career for that kind of life?" She snorted in disgust. "I love her. We all love her in spite of her one-track mind. But some days I wish I were an orphan." She wandered out of the room, muttering.

Lorelei sank down on the bed, vaguely surprised at how calm she felt about the impending visit. Normally, she would be wishing she had a bolt hole for the duration. Pitying looks, veiled references to her "loss," and lip-service interest in her career were not easy to swallow in small doses, but in the giant portions handed out by her family, the situation was impossible.

Pippa poked her head back in the door. "You aren't worrying, are you?" she demanded, studying Lorelei carefully. "Since you've been seeing Alex I thought you were coming to terms with getting out and about. Was I wrong?"

"No. Alex has helped me see that it's time to let go of the past. Between the two of you, if I'm not careful, I could end up with an ego problem." She got to her feet to give Pippa a hug. "Thank you for caring."

"What brought that on?"

"I'm growing up at last. I think I lost more in that accident than the easy use of my leg or my voice. I think somewhere along the line I stopped maturing emotionally. It was as if I were safe as long as I didn't let anyone get too close. I took what you did for me almost as my right. I hid out here and didn't let anyone get near me. I watched you worrying about me in silence and never made any effort to tell you how important you are to me. I let you shower me with love, but I returned precious little to you." Tears welled in her eyes. "If it hadn't been for you I wouldn't have made it this far."

Pippa stared at Lorelei, stunned at the confession. "Oh, honey . . ." she whispered, tears in her own eyes. "I didn't do all that much. I gave you a place to run to and Mystic, but you gave me something, too. I was alone until you came. Besides Jason, you're the only person in this family of ours that hasn't put down my writing. You care about what I do and you don't criticize my weird clothes or my need to break out periodically.

All my life I've been an odd duck in the nest, doing things that drove my parents and siblings wild, needing something that I couldn't explain, wanting to race myself to the edges of the universe. No one accepted me, no one understood. No one would listen when I tried to explain. You did.''

Understanding her aunt more than she ever had before, Lorelei felt the burden of her own conscience ease. She leaned back, unmindful of the tears trickling down her chin. ''Looks like we did ourselves a good turn when we became housemates,'' she teased huskily.

Pippa tipped back her head, laughing heartily. ''That we did. And now we have another to add to our little group. Your Alex.''

Lorelei grinned, feeling younger than she had in years. ''I don't know about the 'your' part, but Alex is definitely a fan of ours. He likes your clothes, says they're fascinating, and he's even read your stories.''

Pippa started down the hall with Lorelei following. ''Thought the man had taste. Nice to know I haven't lost my ability to judge character. I wonder what Gail will make of him?''

Lorelei paused at the head of the stairs. ''She isn't going to make anything of him. Do you think I am going to start a problem by introducing them? I can just see my mother now. Poor little Lorelei. We were so sorry when she got injured. Things have never been the same for her. We are thrilled you can see what a wonderful girl she is in spite of that terrible limp. And I don't think her voice is all that bad. A little rough in the mornings perhaps." She grimaced at the thought of the little unintentional digs with which her mother could spice the conversation.

Pippa turned, eyeing Lorelei sharply. "You really think you're going to be able to convince Alex to stay away from you for two days? I don't. You and that man have been together almost every hour for the last week. I can't see him bowing out for anything less than a major catastrophe, and even then I'm not sure he wouldn't find a way around it. Look at you now. If you hadn't been so stubborn about going to Atlanta with him, you'd be there right this minute."

"I told you his business would take up all his time and I'd end up in his apartment staring at the walls. Besides, as you pointed out, we have been together all week. I'm behind on this game. I'm using these two days to catch up."

A small lie, but Pippa wouldn't know she had done very little with her prince and his lady. All her fantasies seemed centered on one man, one face. Alex. He painted vivid pictures in her waking and sleeping hours. He filled her mind so completely it was almost impossible to remember the simplest things. She missed him with a pain she hadn't expected and even now wasn't sure how to deal with.

"I still say you don't know the man very well

if you think he's going to stay away from you while Gail and her group are here.''

"You want me to do what?" Alex demanded incredulously.

Lorelei remembered Pippa's words and grimaced in disgust at her own inaccurate reading of Alex's reaction. The last thing she wanted was to fight with Alex on his first day back. "I told you what my family is like. My mother will spend her time listing my virtues while all the time underlining how flawed I am. My father will greet you as if you are my last chance at a normal life. If we aren't very careful it won't be just Eugene getting married.''

Alex paced his den, hearing ten words for every one Lorelei spoke. "I am perfectly capable of avoiding being backed in a corner by your parents. The point is, do you want me to meet them? Are you ashamed of our relationship?"

Horrified at his thinking, Lorelei hurried to his side, her eyes wide with shock. "How can you say such a thing?"

He half turned, ignoring her outstretched hand. All the emotions that had been growing within him found expression at last. He wanted to be more to Lorelei than the man who had taught her passion. "I can say it because it could be true. Except for that first night we spent together, you always have to go home after we make love. How do you think I feel being left like that night after night? I asked you to come to Atlanta with me. You didn't even hesitate before you refused.'' The hurt he had felt sharpened his voice. ''You know by now I would never demand anything of you, either emotionally or physically, that you weren't capable of giving. Yet you gave me some weak excuse that we had been doing so much lately that you were tired and needed to rest. How many times were you out on Mystic while I was gone?''

''Four,'' she replied without thinking.

He nodded. ''Two days gone and you rode four times. Resting, Lorelei?''

Her hands dropped at her sides as she stared at him. She had never heard him use such a harsh tone with her before. ''I was restless.'' She saw the flicker in his eyes and for one instant felt a faint softening in his attitude before it was gone.

''Why?''

The question fell like a sword between them. Silence so thick that even the night creatures outside must have felt and been smothered by it surrounded them in an invisible cocoon. For the first time she recognized the depth of his hurt at her refusal to go to the city with him. Confused, bewildered by the guilt she hadn't expected, Lorelei backed away.

His lips twisted at the gesture. ''You know something?'' he asked bitterly. ''All the time I was gone I kept hoping you would use the number I left with you. I wanted you to make the first move out of bed just this once. I needed to know

I was more to you than the first man to show you sensual pleasure. I waited, not sleeping, either, and you didn't call. I walked in here tonight and you weren't here although you knew when I was due back and you had a key. I had to call you." He sighed deeply and glanced out the window. "Maybe I expect too much. Maybe I want too much."

Lorelei stared at his back, realizing how her actions must have seemed to him. Through the tangle of emotions, she knew she could not let him go on believing that it was only passion that held her. "I wanted to call you," she whispered. "I lay awake those two nights wanting to have you hold me . . ." She caught his flinch and bit her lip before plunging on. "It wasn't just desire that made me ache for you. It was knowing you were beside me, listening, talking, or just being silent. I was missing the sharing, of not being lonely, of not reaching out and finding emptiness. I ne—" She stumbled, her voice breaking.

He turned at the sound, reading the need to speak in her eyes and the pain of her failure to make her voice obey her. He reached out, drawing her close, unable to keep his own hurt at the expense of hers. He leaned his cheek against her hair. "You needed me?" Her nod was immediate, stirring the curls so they caressed his lips, teasing them as Lorelei so often had over the last week. "Thank God, woman." His arms tightened as he tried to draw her closer. "I needed you so much.

Those damn negotiations took forever. I wanted to come back here so badly. I needed that peace that you carry around with you. I didn't eat right and I sure as hell didn't sleep right. The phone didn't ring and I had visions of you out with someone else or hurt because you had that stallion out in the dark and had gotten thrown. I never knew my imagination could be so vivid.''

Lorelei raised her head, her hand going to his face, tracing the lines etched in the taut skin. "There is no one else. I never thought of that. And I didn't ride at night. I promised, remember?"

He searched her eyes, seeing the truth. "Don't shut me out again. I have worked all my life to reach for things. I've gotten everything I wanted and more. But I didn't *need* them the way I need you. Let me into your life. You don't have to go to Atlanta or anywhere else you don't want to go. But don't make me pretend we aren't a pair. Let me meet your family.''

Lorelei felt something shatter inside her. Warmth flowed where there had been only cold. His arms were strong and sure. His eyes held promises that he would not force on her. "All right." The relief in his eyes brought tears to hers. "I didn't know how I could face them alone without getting caught in all the old feelings of inadequacy. I didn't want that. You've taught me to stop seeing myself as crippled. I didn't want to forget that even for a second. With you beside me I know I won't forget.''

"You're stronger than you think, my siren lady, but I am glad you need me." If there was a niggling feeling of something not right, he ignored it in his need to touch her. His head bent, his lips took hers with all the pent-up passion that had been his cross to bear while he was away from her.

Lorelei met him halfway, as eager as he to taste the magic that they made together. The future was settled for now. With Alex beside her, her scars had no importance and the people who saw them had no power to hurt her.

# ELEVEN

Alex stood at the window, his back to Lorelei as she lay sleeping in his bed. Dawn was breaking, and this time he was not alone wondering if Lorelei regretted the passion they had shared. He glanced at her, her face softly flushed, her lips slightly parted. The sheet draped across her breasts and hips, leaving her limbs bare. Her scars were visible, but he didn't notice them. To him she was more than a lovely curved body. Her mind, her serenity, her gentleness and passion were the ties that bound him to her. He stirred, feeling the desire build slowly, deepening his breathing, bringing memories—and more. A need that had nothing to do with physical fulfillment beckoned him to the bed. He knelt beside her, his hands slipping beneath her to raise her in his arms. Her lashes fluttered open, her eyes gradually focusing on his face. A smile was born on her lips. He bent to share his own with her in a gentle kiss.

"I love the way you wake me," Lorelei whispered, stretching sensuously against him.

"And I love having you in my arms and in my bed," he replied huskily. He eased down beside her to fit her body to his. "Tell me you don't have to work today. I want to spend the hours with you. Ride, have a picnic, or just laze around here. Maybe even drive into town." He smoothed the curve of her shoulder, his fingers gliding down to the ivory fullness of her breast.

Lorelei gasped at the caress. The fire of his touch was warming her, building the tension that she had come to know so well. "I'm not quite finished with the game," she protested half-heartedly.

"How much more?"

"I need to run it through with someone. I usually wait for Pippa to test-run them for me, but she's busy with her book."

"Then let me."

Lorelei lifted her head, her eyes widening with surprise. "Are you serious?"

"Of course. Didn't I almost beat you at the arcade? I'm not quite as quick as you, but I'm not all that bad."

"It could take hours depending on how caught up in the maze you get," she warned. Eagerness to share this part of her life grew.

"I want to see your creation. In fact, I would consider it an honor to give it a trial run." He tucked a lock of dark hair behind her ear. The tears in Lorelei's eyes surprised him. "What's wrong, honey?"

Lorelei smiled mistily. "Did I tell you what a wonderful man you are?"

Relieved at her expression and her words, he grinned and pulled her on top of him. "Not in the last five minutes. Not that I'm complaining, mind you, but a man does like to be appreciated."

"Does a man now?" Lorelei teased, feeling the hardness nudging at the heart of her own desire. She rotated her hips, tantalizing Alex with each controlled swing.

Alex groaned. "Woman, you ought to be outlawed. I don't think those coaches of yours had this in mind when they taught you how to use that delectable little body of yours."

Lorelei bent her head, nipping at his lips. "You don't like?"

"I like it so much you may just kill me with pleasure." He captured her mouth with a hot demand that he could no longer restrain.

Lorelei responded instantly. Her fingers threaded through his hair as her tongue dueled with his. Her groan found its echo in his as Alex joined them as one. The dawn turned into morning but neither noticed, the fire between them so strong that nothing could penetrate the passion they created.

\*　　\*　　\*

"So tell me about your family," Alex invited. He leaned back against the tree and stared out over the lake. The horses were tethered off to one side. The blanket on which they had shared a picnic lunch made the hard ground a little less so.

Lorelei turned her head, her eyes tracing Alex's strong profile. The sun gilded his hair with gold and painted arresting shadows over his body. Love crept softly out of the dark corners of her mind, drawn by the light and the man who sat beside her. Her skin paled as she stared at him. She had not expected love, had not known she could feel it.

Alex turned and caught the strange, confused look in her eyes. He reached out to touch her cheek. "Tell me. What is it? Your family? Did I tread on dangerous ground with my question?"

Lorelei covered his hand with hers, pressing his warmth against her skin. She tried a smile, hoping it looked more natural than it felt. "No, my mind is off in a cloud," she murmured, willing him to be satisfied with her answer. She didn't know what to do. Nothing in her life had prepared her for this.

Alex studied her for a moment. Lorelei regretted the lie even as she hid behind it. She released a careful sigh of relief as his face cleared. "All right, give. Tell me all about your family. I want to know them.'' He pulled her close, tucking her comfortably against his side.

Lorelei relaxed, savoring the tenderness of the gesture. She loved it when Alex touched her for no reason other than liking to have her close. Her family was not given to affectionate displays. Alex's need to reach out to her was becoming more important each day and never more so than now. She loved him. She might not know what to do with the knowledge but that didn't stop her from whispering the words in her mind and savoring the strength it gave her.

''I have four brothers. Eugene is the youngest and Jason is the oldest. Between them are Gary and Bob.''

''Were you close to any of them?''

Lorelei frowned at the question, never having considered it before. ''To Jason, I guess. In fact . . .'' She paused as she remembered his visit to the hospital right after she had been told she would never compete again and would be very fortunate if she walked.

Alex waited, sensing more behind her hesitation than the telling of a few facts.

''Jason came to me on the darkest night of my life. He held my hand while I screamed in rage and pain and wouldn't let the doctors drug me. He listened when everyone else said it was normal to feel like destroying things. He let me pour out all the ugliness I had bottled up after the accident, and he never said one word in judgment. Then when I was done, he did a really strange thing. He smiled at me." She raised her head, grinning at Alex's frown. "You'd have to know Jason to realize the gift of his smile. He is probably one of the coldest men alive. I can count on one hand the times I have seen him touched by emotion. But he was that night. He told me I shouldn't listen to all the medical hype. I should listen to my body. It knew it could walk and when. It knew I was only using a part of its potential and it was telling me it was time to start using the whole. And more than that, Jason told me that I had the heart and the guts to make my body work if I wanted to. The choice was mine. Then he reached through all the tubes they had attached to me and put his hand on my heart. He looked in my eyes and said: 'As long as this works, you can do anything you want to do bad enough. Go for it, kid.' "

Lorelei shook her head as the memory departed. "I learned later that he had just skated in a competition on the East Coast and had flown all day to get to me and had to be back the following morning for the rest of the ice-skating meet. He won. The papers said he skated one of the most coldly brilliant performances of his life. My parents were ecstatic and hardly noticed that Pippa had arrived for her first visit. To this day I swear Jason called her. The two of them have always been close, although I don't know why. You couldn't find two people farther apart in personality."

"Will I meet Jason this weekend?"

"No. Just Mom and Dad, Eugene, his girl, and her family. Pippa has been muttering about the woman wanting to look us over to be sure there are no genetic defects. She's been threatening to pretend to be unhinged or something equally dramatic. When I went to tell her you and I would be out today, I found her knee-deep in her closet yanking out all her most outrageous outfits trying to decide what she'll wear when they arrive."

Alex laughed deeply, easily picturing the scene. "I hope you didn't stop her. I want to see her in her finery."

Lorelei giggled. "I couldn't have stopped her if I tried. She and my mother seem to bring out the worst in each other. It will be a tossup to see whose temper breaks first."

"You sound like you aren't dreading this visit."

"I'm not, or at least not so much," she admitted. She turned in his arms, meeting his eyes. "Because of you I'm learning not to mind what people see when they look at me."

"What they see is a beautiful woman."

She smiled. "Until you, no one ever told me that before." Love filled her heart as she looked at him. She wasn't sure what he felt for her. Desire surely. Passion definitely. Need, too. But love? Despite his gentleness and tenderness, he had never said the words. Her new confidence was growing by the day, but it was not strong enough to enable her to say three little words. So she kept silent, hugging her secret to herself, unworried about the future in the brightness of the present.

Lorelei put the finishing touches on her makeup and studied herself in the mirror. No, her family probably wouldn't notice anything different about her, she decided. Her love for Alex wasn't written on her face. Pleased with the image she presented in dark-green slacks and pale-pink blouse she smiled at her slim reflection before turning from the mirror to head for the door. Now if only Pippa had bowed to the voice of reason and opted for one of her less spectacular ensembles. She knocked on her aunt's door, just barely controlling an urgent need to laugh aloud when she got her first look at Pippa's costume. Her aunt had really outdone herself this time. She had a multitude of rainbow-hued drapes that were probably intended to be some sort of at-home lounging outfit. It succeeded in drawing the eye, making the viewer devoutly wish for a pair of sunglasses.

"Do you like it?" Pippa preened, her eyes gleaming brighter than her dress.

"It's definitely different," Lorelei said faintly.

"Good," Pippa returned just as the doorbell sounded. "I hope that's Alex and not the horrible horde."

"Pippa, promise me you won't get my mother started. I know you like kicking at the traces of her rigidity but not this weekend," Lorelei pleaded.

Pippa turned from the mirror, all humor gone

from her face. "Honey, did it ever occur to you that when your mother is griping at me she doesn't have time to pick at anyone else?"

Stunned at the reasoning, Lorelei stared. "You do it for that reason?"

"Sometimes."

"For me?"

"Sometimes."

"I never realized."

"You were hurting. I couldn't let them do any more damage. They might mean well with their little digs, but those darts can go right to the heart. I drew their fire."

Lorelei shook her head, finding another example of how blind she had been to the world around her.

The bell pealed again. "Your Alex is getting impatient. You'd better go."

"But I don't need you to protect me anymore."

Pippa smiled complacently. "I know. This time is just for me." Her expression darkened, a wicked look in her eyes. "Gail messed with my writing once too often."

"You look like you've just stumbled through the looking glass," Alex murmured as he studied Lorelei's frowning expression.

"I feel like it," she admitted wryly.

"What happened? Something I can help with?"

"I just found out that Pippa has been using those crazy clothes of hers for reasons other than just because she likes being outrageous. She's been bugging my mother for years every time she makes one of her duty stops.''

"As long as your mother was carping at Pippa she would leave you alone," Alex guessed.

Lorelei blinked, startled at his perception. "How did you figure that out?''

"Stands to reason. Your aunt loves you." He could have added that Lorelei seemed so fragile that anyone with any sensitivity at all would do their utmost to protect her from hurt. Hadn't he found the power of her delicate aura in his own need to keep her safe?

She had never admired weak, clingy women, and to know she had been skirting the edge of becoming one angered her. "But I don't need that now.''

Alex took her in his arms, kissing her lightly. "A little extra insurance never hurt anyone.''

Lorelei softened against him, forgetting her temper. "I don't want to hide anymore.''

"You aren't.''

Pippa paused at the top of the stairs to survey the embracing pair. "Unless you two want to be marching down the aisle with Eugene you better break it up," Pippa said, waving an arm decked out in an extravagant array of bracelets. "They're here.''

The sounds of a car pulling into the drive followed by doors shutting reached their ears. Alex bent his head, taking one more taste of Lorelei's lips to tide him over. "All right, beautiful, let's meet your clan," he whispered before releasing her. Threading his fingers with hers, he gave her hand a squeeze.

Lorelei looked down at their linked hands and knew that the days of hiding anything were almost over. This morning she had cared that her family not find out about Alex. Now she was beginning to know she could not demean what they shared by trying to pretend they weren't lovers. It was time she had acknowledged to others that she was a woman with a right to her own life, not a crippled being. She breathed deeply, fighting the need to retreat as she had in the past. It was time to be strong, and with Alex beside her she felt she could face even her well-meaning but critical family. She made herself smile and lifted his hand to her lips. The relief in his eyes was plain. Her love grew stronger that he cared so much. The doorbell rang and the weekend she should have dreaded began.

Alex watched Lorelei's family, more interested in viewing their reactions to Lorelei than his own introduction. Lorelei's responses had their roots in these people and the way they had handled her accident. To understand them was to deepen his understanding of Lorelei.

"Darling, you are looking so much better than the last time we saw you. Your limp hardly shows at all these days," Gail greeted her daughter, beaming proudly. She turned to the artfully blond woman at her side and introduced the Bakers. "We are all so proud of our little Lori. She really put herself back together so well," she told the group.

The blond woman nodded, and Alex found himself besieged by an urgent need to wring Lorelei's mother's neck. Of all the tactless things to say to a bunch of strangers. His hand tightened around Lorelei's fingers as he felt her stiffen beside him. He wanted to lift Lorelei into his arms and carry her from the stares that were now directed at her leg and body.

Lorelei fought the need to run, feeling the familiar desire to apologize for not being whole steal some of her confidence. Remembering Alex and all the things he had taught her helped keep her smile intact although it frayed around the edges.

"Gail, you have the most extraordinary way of putting a damper on things," Pippa announced curtly, floating toward the group, her drapes fluttering like angry bird wings. "Come into the living room. Stop picking at Lorelei before I forget I'm a lady." She hissed the last sentence so that only her sister could hear. She directed a false smile at the rest of the guests and led the way. "So this is your little fiancée, Eugene," she murmured, arranging herself dramatically against the backdrop of the fireplace.

Lorelei started to follow the exodus but Alex

stopped her. "Are you all right?" He touched her cheek, frowning at the paleness of her skin.

"I'm fine, but I'll be glad when they leave. Mother is in her usual form." She leaned into his caress, taking strength from his warmth and the glow in his eyes.

"She's right about one thing, you know. Your limp *is* better. So put that chin up and don't let them get to you." He traced the outline of her lips. "Now let's mount a rescue before Pippa has their hearts on a platter." His eyes narrowed on the shaky grin that trembled against his thumb. The serenity he had always associated with Lorelei was gone. Tension was in her limbs and fear mixed with self-doubt was back in her eyes. His anger deepened at the insensitivity of her family. Not one of them but Pippa had tried to spare Lorelei her mother's tongue. He tucked her hand in the crook of his arm, ready to join battle with Pippa for Lorelei's sake.

By late afternoon, Alex had had all he could take. Watching Lorelei wilt before his eyes hurt more than anything ever had in his life. Every bit of confidence that he had seen growing in her was gone. Of the three of her relatives present—her mother, father, and brother—not one had missed an opportunity to somehow put a negative gloss on her physical abilities, her career, and her lifestyle. The horror of it was that not once could he find one hint of maliciousness in anything any of them did. They smothered Lorelei, treating her almost as a backward, barely functioning child, and it wasn't long before the Bakers were following suit. He paced the terrace thinking hard as he waited for Lorelei to join him. Lunch was finished and everyone but he and Lorelei had gone down to the stables to see Mystic. Lorelei had gone to her room to freshen up. A sound alerted him that he was no longer alone. He turned to find her framed in the doorway, looking so much like the silent, wary creature he had stumbled upon in the woods that he felt pain at the transition. Suddenly, he couldn't look at her without needing an outlet for his frustration.

"Well, what happens now? Has your lovely family got any more barbs hidden up their collective sleeves?"

Lorelei limped forward, more tired than she could remember being in a long time. "I'm sorry they've given you such a hard time. I knew they would be difficult, but I never expected my father to grill you about your business and I certainly never thought Eugene could ask you if you had known me before I was injured."

Alex shrugged away her concern. "That wasn't what I was talking about. I want to know if this is the way they always are when they visit. I have wondered why your need to hide is so extreme. Now I know. I'm surprised you ever let anyone see you if this is how they all acted when you were hurt."

It was Lorelei's turn to shrug. "Jason didn't

carry on like the others. He's much the same as you and Pippa.'' She sighed, feeling older by the moment as she limped to his side. ''I truly thought it would be better this time. I thought they would see that I was happy and really getting on with my life.''

''You mean because of me?'' He watched her intently, a sudden unpalatable thought entering his mind. Anger, fear, and bitterness stirred, surprising him. ''You didn't let me meet your family for us. You wanted me here as a buffer, maybe even as protection,'' he said, taking a shot in the dark as to her motives. Wanting to protect her and knowing that she needed him to protect her to survive were two different things. His life was demanding. Unless Lorelei was strong emotionally and mentally, their relationship would never survive. They could work around her physical limitations—but not the rest.

Hesitating, Lorelei froze, caught by the confusion of emotion building in his eyes. ''It wasn't like that.''

''Then tell me how it was. Have you gotten so used to someone taking up for you that you have come to depend on it. I thought you brave. Was I wrong? Are you using me?'' he demanded.

Lorelei inhaled sharply, drawing back a step, knowing at least part of what he said was true. She had needed him to give her the strength to try.

He caught her arms, betrayal an acid taste in his mouth. "Answer me," he bit out.

"I needed you here. Was that so wrong?"

"Why?" He refused to be swayed by the truth in her voice. He wanted more—the reasons behind the truth.

Lorelei struggled, trying to free herself. His touch, his words demanded more than she wanted to face. She was gasping when she finally realized her struggles were useless. She sagged in his arms, her eyes locked with his. There was no mercy now, no quarter to be given. "I love you," she said, half in defiance and half in fear of rejection.

Alex stared at her, the declaration cutting like a knife to the heart of all that he had tried to hide from himself. This was why he had cared so passionately. This was why he could not work without thinking of Lorelei. This was why, that even now, he couldn't handle the fact that she could not make a stand against her family for all their subtle putdowns.

"The woman I could and do love has courage and strength. She wouldn't cringe like a beaten cat every time someone looked at her. She wouldn't hide in the shadows for fear. She wouldn't let her intelligence be labeled an amusing hobby. She would fight for herself and for me. I need you, Lorelei. But I would never offer you less than the whole of me and I don't want less than the whole of you. The damage that accident did to you wasn't just to your body. It was to your mind.

Even now you're afraid to live, to be the whole woman that you are." His anger died at the confusion in her eyes. Defeat was bitter. He hadn't expected it, hadn't known he would be fighting this battle, hadn't realized the depth of his commitment until it was too late. He, who hadn't been certain love existed, had discovered just how strong a force within himself it was.

"I want it all or nothing, and in return I'll give you everything that is in me. The choice is yours." He released her and stepped back, hoping she would say something, knowing in his heart she didn't understand him, maybe never would. "I'm going home. Come to me there if you find you can share the same feelings for me that I want to give you. Come to me only if you are prepared to accept life and make a commitment." His lips twisted into a grim smile. "I could promise I will wait forever but I won't ever lie to you. I'm a man, not a hero. I need my woman, you, in my life. But if you can't or won't come, I'll survive. And it won't be by hiding in the dark and pretending you never touched me. You've given me something, whether you know it or not. I've learned what's important and what's not. I've learned when to fight and when to give in. This is the moment to bow to superior forces. I can't fight your battles for you. You alone must do that."

# TWELVE

Lorelei wasn't conscious of moving down the path leading to the garden at the back edge of the property. She needed time alone and there was no better place than Pippa's exotic plant collection. No one would think to look for her there. Tears stung her eyes as she dropped onto the bench near a small pond. Alex's harsh words beat an unrelenting tattoo in her mind. Had she let him meet her family to use him as a buffer? Had she become so paranoid that she needed that kind of a crutch? How would she have felt if he had used her the same way? Hurt? Angry? Betrayed?

She loved him. She had drawn her strength from him. Was that right or yet another act of a fearridden woman? She had enjoyed herself when she had gone out with Alex. No one had treated her as a deficient being then. Had she been drawn into crediting his presence with the way she was so readily accepted? For the first time in her life she stopped thinking like the injured seventeen-year-old child she had once been and used the intelligence of the woman she had become. Her chin lifted, the slump of her shoulders straightened, her tears dried.

"Damn!" she swore aloud, all the pent-up emotion of nine long years of subtle growing and maturing in the one word. The child who had gone through more operations than she wanted to remember and survived had become a woman with grit to fight for what she wanted. And she wanted Alex. She loved Alex. But first she had to prove to herself and to him that she had healed, that the past was gone, and that the scars were badges of her own courage and not labels of loss. She rose, knowing exactly where and with whom she would start.

She was halfway up the path when she met Pippa coming to look for her.

"Are you all right?" Pippa demanded, blocking the path as she searched Lorelei's face.

Lorelei grinned, her eyes bright with power and determination. "I love you, Pippa, but from this moment on you will never need to ask me that question again. I am fine. Much as your protection has meant to me all these years I don't need it anymore." She touched Pippa's arm, not wanting to hurt her as she made her first declaration of independence. "I can never tell you how much you have done for me and I can never repay your love and caring, but I've found my feet at last."

The two women faced each other silently, bonds forged of love and need stretching between them. Then Pippa's grin broke the mood, her eyes gleaming wickedly. "Would this have anything to do with that very angry man who stomped out of my house a while ago?"

"You bet your favorite scandalous outfit it does," Lorelei laughed. "He's so mad at me, I'm going to have a hard time convincing him that I have grown up. I don't care because I will win. But before I tackle him I've got a few other people to set straight."

"Hurray. May I come and watch?"

"You would even if I said no," Lorelei said ruefully as Pippa let her pass.

"Darn straight. I've been waiting years for someone to put a flea in Gail's ear. I knew you had it in you." Pippa's scarves flapped about her as she strode up the walk. "Bet you any amount of money she turns purple when you face her down."

Lorelei found a chuckle bubbling up as she entered the living room where she found only her parents present. Gail glanced up, her polite smile dying as she surveyed Lorelei.

"Darling, don't you think you should have had a rest while we were gone? We wouldn't want you to get tired because of all the activity."

"Actually, Mother, the walk did me good, although a ride would have been even better."

"Perhaps, dear, but it has been a long day for you and there is still dinner to get through," Gail pointed out.

"Mother, I have had longer days. Not only that, but believe it or not, lately I've even managed to go out dancing, playing games in a video arcade, and wandering around town just window-shopping," Lorelei said, suddenly feeling deliciously free. She ambled across the room, realizing her leg was no longer as tired and weak as it had been earlier. She sat down and found everyone watching her.

"Contrary to popular belief, at least in this family, I am not an invalid. There are things I can't do, but then that's true for most people. I am tired of feeling I have to apologize for a few scars and a tiny limp."

Her words fell into a pool of silence. Lorelei surveyed the various expressions turned her way and knew that Alex would be proud of her but no prouder of her than she was of herself.

"We haven't treated you as an invalid. And we are very pleased at how adept you have become. But you must admit you do have to take care," Gail said defensively, finally finding her voice.

"I'm sorry, Mother, but you have treated me just that way. Every time I see you, you spend every moment reminding me of the way I used to be. That was nine years ago. A long time in anyone's life. I didn't win the medal and I didn't turn out like the rest of you, but I'm not doing badly for myself. You never see that or if you do, it doesn't mean anything to you. I can't handle that anymore.''

"Lorelei!" Lorelei's father gasped in shock at her behavior. "I don't know what's come over you."

"I've grown up, Dad. It's about time, don't you think?"

He stared at her, his face mirroring his confusion. "Have we really been that bad?" he asked oddly, his superbly conditioned body braced as if to take a punch.

Lorelei closed the distance between them and laid her hand on his arm. "I'm afraid so, but it hasn't been all your fault. I let you treat me this way."

He lifted his hand to her shoulder, awkwardly patting it. "We love you."

Lorelei smiled faintly. "I know. I love you, too."

Gail took a step toward them, even more unaccustomed to affectionate displays than her husband. "I didn't know," she murmured. "I didn't mean to hurt you. I worry." She spread her hands, suddenly looking old and not as strong as usual.

Lorelei felt her pity stir, just now beginning to realize the cost of her injuries to those who had to watch her suffer and who in their own way had lost as much as she. "Mother, I would have done my best to be a champion. I wanted that medal as much, if not more, than you. That's over now. We have to accept I have a new life now, a whole new life.''

''With that man?''

Her smile widened. ''If I'm really lucky.''

''I liked him, honey,'' her father said gruffly. He glanced significantly at his wife.

She nodded and added, ''So did I.''

''I'm glad, but believe it or not, it wouldn't have mattered if you hadn't liked him. We belong together.'' Her love strengthened and redoubled at the declaration. Her eyes shone with life and a power that she was just beginning to realize.

''Hurray!'' Pippa clapped her hands, beaming at them as though the reconciliation was all her doing. Gail glared. Her husband grunted, and Lorelei escaped the scene, feeling oddly amused at the family squabbling. Her limp was hardly noticeable as she let herself out of the kitchen door and hurried down the path to the stables. The decision to take Mystic instead of the car wasn't a conscious one, nor was the fact that she found herself taking the longer route through the woods to get to Alex's house. There was no room for surprise when she entered the thicket and found Alex sitting on the boulder in almost the same position as the first time she had seen him. She drew rein to watch him. Her scarf was draped across his lap, his eyes steady on hers.

Alex gazed at her, seeing the bold look in her

eyes he had always longed for. The tension of knowing that their future hung in the balance left his body in one long sigh of relief. She couldn't look like that and come to tell him that they were finished. He wanted to go to her, but this time she had to make the first move. It was important for her and for their relationship. She had to know her strength as a woman, the woman he loved, and as a person. He wouldn't steal an instant of that realization from her to ease the pain of his need to hold her, to have a commitment to last a lifetime from her lips.

"Say something," Lorelei demanded, unable to bear the silence a moment longer.

He shook his head, suddenly knowing that it was his turn to be the one cloaked in silence.

Lorelei eased Mystic closer, feeling her muscles clench on this new hurdle. Telling her family of the changes in her had been easier than this. "You were right and I was wrong. I did use you," she admitted in a rush, needing to get the confession out of the way so she could get on with what she really wanted to say.

Alex stroked the silk scarf, waiting.

Lorelei moved Mystic even closer, challenged by his silence. "I told them. My parents, I mean. I told them what they were doing to me. When I did, I saw that most of the fault lay with me. If I wasn't strong enough to stand up for myself I deserved to be treated as a dim-witted child." Still he didn't speak. Frustration overpowered the challenge. Anger built. Lorelei slid from the saddle, dropping the reins to the ground as she walked toward him. "Say something."

He shook his head.

"Why not?"

He pointed to her.

"Me first."

He nodded.

"There isn't anything else," she muttered, casting her mind around for what could be missing.

One brow quirked at her tone, but he remained mute.

"This isn't fair." She felt on the verge of stamping her foot as she stopped before him. The hidden laughter and longing in his eyes were the spurs to whatever inhibitions she still possessed. Without thinking, she pulled the scarf from his grasp and took his hands and placed them around her waist. Catching his face in her palms, she kissed him, putting every ounce of love and determination she had in the meeting of their lips. His mouth softened beneath hers but did not open. Needing him, wanting him, she traced his lips with her tongue. He repeated the caress. She nudged at his lips. He did the same.

Lorelei lifted her head, finally understanding. "I only get as much as I give," she stated, and without waiting for an answer, she lowered her head again. Just before her mouth took his, she whispered, "I hope I fry your heart from the inside out, my love."

Lorelei pressed closer as she turned up the heat of passion, the fire burning within her. She felt Alex's shiver of response and gloried in the knowledge that she had the ability to steal his control. The sweet duel of their mouths had no winner only mutual recipients of pleasure. Her fingers slipped down his chest, pulling apart his shirt in her need to feel more of his warmth. A moment later she felt the cool air touch her skin as he bared her breasts. She lifted her head, breathing in soft pants. His laughter was rough yet strangely tender.

"Woman, you are some kind of lover, but do you really want to make love here?"

"I don't care. I want you. I want to be part of you and I want you to be a part of me."

His eyes darkened, his body going taut. "Then let's go home where I can do the deed properly." He rose, cradling her against his chest.

Lorelei wrapped her arms around his neck, her lips nibbling at his throat as he carried her to Mystic.

"Behave yourself or I won't make an honest woman of you," he threatened.

"An honest woman of me!" She raised her eyes, giving him a mock glare. "What a sexist remark. Maybe I don't want to be an honest woman."

"Then no loving." He plopped her gently on top of the stallion before swinging less gracefully up behind her.

"Alex! Who died and made you king?" she demanded as he took the reins and headed the horse down the path toward his house.

"You did by coming to me that way. By giving yourself to me. By taking me as I am, temper and workaholic disposition and all."

"I still want a proposal, a real proposal," she protested. She gasped as his hand cupped her breast, teasing the erect peak.

He stared down at her soft body curled against his. "You can't mean what I think you mean. Are you talking about one of those get-on-your-knees varieties?"

"You bet your sweet body I am. I want the whole works." She leaned back so that she could see his face. The male scowl at the pomp of the traditional hand-seeking made her laugh.

His eyes gleamed as he kissed her deeply, breathlessly. "I think I created a greedy woman," he complained halfheartedly as he lifted his head.

"Helped create," she corrected. "I did part of the work myself."

His amusement died and a deep feeling of satisfaction filled him. "That you did, love. That you did. I wanted so much to be there when you spread your wings . . ."

Lorelei covered his lips with her fingers, stilling his words. "It was better that you left me. It was only then that I could see what I needed to do. You will never know how much your belief in me meant."

He kissed her fingers, smiling at her, proud that she had chosen him in spite of all the obstacles that had stood in their way. "I hope our children have your courage."

His smile became hers, the love in her eyes more eloquent than any words would ever be. "And your faith and perception."

He hugged her tightly as he kicked Mystic into a slow canter. "Let's go home so we can start the rest of our lives."